8TH

Vol.1

RaShodd Dancy

8th Vol.1

Copyright © 2021 by RaShodd Dancy

The following is a complete work of fiction. Any names, places, symbols, logos, characters are a complete product of the authors imagination. Any resemblance to persons dead or alive is entirely coincidental.

ISBN: 9780578914367

ISBN: 9780578914350

info@Rebirthproductions.org

To My Dad Ray and aunt Luella.

Prologue

"I love you," she whispered to the baby in her arms.

He stared up at her with sweet, trusting eyes and she felt warmth radiating through the physical construct she was inhabiting. Almost immediately, though, her sorrow increased.

The parting would be hard, mostly on her. She had already stayed so much longer than she intended. There was the pregnancy and then the last three months. Every day was new and wonderful, bringing with it some unexpected surprise.

That was the best part of all. She'd long ago given up the notion of finding something new in the universe. Everything always played out the same whether a year or ten thousand had passed.

In a few hours the physical construct, Jenna, would awake to realize that she had lost time. How Jenna would react was uncertain, but she had prepared and left her videos of memories that weren't Jenna's but could have been.

The baby fussed in her arms and she glanced back down at him. He was so perfect, even if he looked completely normal. That was best for now. He needed to be this way so his guardians would take care of him, love him, and raise him as their own.

The baby, Jaxon, grabbed her finger in his pudgy little fist and squeezed hard. It wasn't nearly as hard as he'd squeezed her finger that first day he had come into the world. That was good. He was absorbing her teaching. He needed to in order to pass.

"It won't always be this way, my darling," she whispered to him.

He cozied up to her.

"We will be together again," she whispered for his ears alone.

There was comprehension in the young eyes that stared up at her. She felt her throat constrict as several emotions vied for control and threatened to overwhelm her. A tear slid down her cheek and Jaxon let go of her finger and stretched his tiny hand up toward the tear as though to wipe it away.

When he touched her face he frowned, his face scrunching up. Then something else happened. It was like watching a ripple beneath the surface of a small pond. Something moved beneath the baby's skin.

She blinked away the tears and stared intently at her son.

There it was again, a small movement at first, so subtle only a mother would have noticed. The skin shifted slightly as something passed under it.

Or was trying to pass through it.

The baby's face shifted, growing swiftly darker. Then it seemed to turn slightly to the side. Suddenly where there were two eyes now there were four. A second nose appeared and a second mouth. Her true son was trying to break free of his vessel and he was about to succeed.

The second face emerged from the skin of the first until the child had two heads. He began to struggle to free himself of the body as well.

"Not yet," she whispered.

She grabbed hold of the emerging child. With her hand she pushed on his neck and after several seconds shoved him back inside his prison. She stuffed the last of him inside. The baby looked serene, whole, again. The only thing to show what had just passed was a bright red mark on his neck in the shape of her thumb.

Even as she watched, the red faded, but the mark remained, darkening to look like a birthmark.

"What am I going to do with you?" she chided gently.

The baby began to cry.

"I know you're impatient, but it's not time yet. You're not ready." She heaved a sigh. "No one is ready."

She could feel him struggling to get out again and she placed her hand over his tiny chest, closed her eyes, and concentrated. Energy flowed from her into the infant, surrounding him in a faint glow. She could feel her son fighting, pushing back, wanting to come out into the world. She held him inside as gently as she could but she was amazed at how strong he was.

He didn't want to be contained. He didn't want to be denied.

But he had to be. Just for now.

She pushed harder, sending the energy spiraling

through the small body she clutched to her breast. It would bind the two together for as long as it needed to.

Until he was truly ready to take his place in the universe.

She began singing a lullaby. It was not one she had sung before, but it seemed to come from deep inside her. Jenna was awakening. The process had begun and while it was not too late to reverse it, it would be unwise to stay any longer than she already had.

So, she sang the lullaby that bubbled up from inside her. It made her heart ache and her eyes burn. The song was meant to soothe but somehow it just made her feel worse.

Like she was abandoning her child.

She took a deep breath, pushing the emotions down deep inside of her even as she had once pushed Jenna down, down deep where there was only darkness and emptiness.

She was not abandoning her child. She would be back,

but for now she had to let him learn and grow on his own. It was important.

The child was still fighting her, but it was growing weaker, succumbing to the energy she was pouring into it. Finally, the *inner* child became still, waiting, watching. He didn't understand. Not yet.

But he would, she told herself.

At last he gave up, resigned to submit to her will, at least for the moment. She staggered slightly, her energy nearly drained after having to suppress his.

It was not the way she would have wished this parting to go, but she was glad he had tried to manifest himself now while she could still take care of it.

She took a shaky breath and wondered if all mothers felt the sting of parting as fiercely as she did. Somehow, she doubted it. How could they, after all?

She sat down slowly in the chair in which she had rocked her baby to sleep many nights. The eyes that looked up at her were those of Jaxon. Her true *inner* son was sleeping for the moment which was good for both of them.

"I am coming back for you. Until then, I will give you something so that you are never alone," she whispered.

With the baby in her lap she took off the necklace she was wearing. It was a seven-point star. She stared at it a long moment. The whole universe had revolved around seven since the beginning. Things were different now. Changed forever.

She held the star in her hand and focused, rallying the last of her reserves. Before her eyes the star began to pulse and shimmer. Then, ever so slowly, a new point began to emerge. When it was half as long as the others she collapsed, nearly overcome by all her efforts.

She felt weak, the body containing her was so limiting. That was one of the reasons she couldn't stay. It had never been meant to hold her for so long.

She put the necklace on the child, knowing that he was

far too aware to choke on it as another baby might.

"This will protect you, comfort you, whisper to you of your greatness until the day which we are reunited," she promised her son.

At last Jaxon, too, was asleep on her lap. Ever so gently she lifted the tiny form, careful not to damage the vessel. She placed him in his crib then stood looking down at him for a moment.

In the next room Julius stirred.

"Hon, you coming to bed?" he called out.

"I'll be right there," she said.

Slowly, deliberately, she shed her clothes as she would soon shed the body that held her. She turned and walked into the bedroom. Jenna would wake in the arms of her husband, though to her mind he would still just be her lover. At least she would find comfort in his presence.

As for her son, she had done everything she could. Now so much was up to him.

"It's all about you, baby," she whispered, willing him to hear this one last message before she left.

Chapter 1

Transcending

June 15, 2018br
City of Angels, Baja California

"On your marks. Set."

The crack of the gun sent a shockwave through Jaxon as he exploded out of the blocks. "Drive, drive, drive." The roar of the crowd filled his ears. "Get tall, get tall, straighten up, knees up, pump those arms." In his peripheral he could see his two friends Sadia and Pete leap to their feet to cheer him on. Jaxon pushed harder and began to run as fast as he could. At a quick glance he looks at the other runners, some keeping an even pace with him, some falling behind. He didn't care about them. All he cared about was the man who was in front of him.

Reggie Rapid, the fastest man alive, was running away from the pack as everyone expected. This was an exhibition race for charity, where any and all were invited to match their speed against his. None were expected to come close. They didn't know Jaxon.

The runner next to Jaxon crashed to the ground, whether a victim of the extreme heat or tripping Jaxon didn't know. He couldn't focus on him or the others. All he could do was focus on Reggie. He had to catch the man who seemed to be pulling farther ahead of the pack.

Relax, allow me to control the chaos. I've got this, just let me take control and we won't have any problems, his *inner* voice purred.

"Yea I suppose," Jaxon muttered back to himself.

"I'm still a little nervous, though."

Don't worry, relax, and enjoy the show.

The *inner* voice had been with him as long as he could remember, the *inner* half, *inner* power, whatever it was. Lately he could feel it growing, it was becoming clearer, stronger, and it decided it wanted to do more.

That was the only reason he was in this race. The other, the *inner* wanted to win. It had something it wanted to prove.

Just breathe in through your nose and out your mouth. I'll handle the rest.

Jaxon hesitated for a moment. He wasn't sure why. Then he let go and everything seemed to click, a new power just flowed through his body.

He could feel his breathing, strong and even. The track began slipping away beneath his feet at an unbelievable speed. There was no fatigue in his muscles, no sensation of strain or effort. Everything felt free and easy.

He surged forward, faster than he'd ever run before. Wind whipped past, causing his eyes to blur, but he didn't slow down. Instead he just went faster and faster. It was like there was no upward limit to how fast he could go. There was a vague realization that he was catching up to Reggie Rapid. A few moments later he was right beside the famous runner.

"Yes, yes, faster! Jaxon," Sadia called out, as Jaxon pulled alongside Reggie.

"Pour it on! You can do it," Pete yelled.

His legs extended, pushing down and back, applying force harder and faster. He was pulling ahead of Reggie. The track in front of him was clear. It was just him ahead of the pack racing alone, and he felt alive, free, in a way that he never felt before.

The tape loomed in front of him, much earlier than it should have. Before he could think of putting on a fresh burst of speed, it broke across his chest. He kept running, but finally started to slow as thoughts began to reenter his brain.

He won the race.

We won!

He beat the fastest man alive.

We are the fastest man alive!

He turned and began to jog back to the finish line just in time to see the last three racers cross it. He was struggling to comprehend what just happened, and then sound came rushing back in.

"A new world record! Unbelievable! A complete unknown dominated the field. Ladies and gentlemen, this is history in the making."

He jogged up to Reggie Rapid who was standing, hands on his knees, breathing deeply. He looked up at Jaxon as he approached and he felt a wave of almost embarrassment. He couldn't quite explain it, but it felt uncomfortable.

"I'm sorry," the words burst out of him before he realized he was going to say them.

Reggie looked surprised and then chuckled.

"Don't ever apologize for being the best at something," he said. "Records are made to be broken."

The other runners walked slowly over to him. Several congratulated Jaxon and patted him on the back. All of them were looking at him with the same awe that he had looked at Reggie with before the start of the race.

The announcer came back on and a hush fell over the stadium.

"Ladies and gentlemen, an update. Since this was a charity event and not an official race, the time is not official. That means Reggie Rapid's record still stands."

There was an audible reaction from the audience.

Reggie looked at Jaxon. "It's okay. Everyone here today knows what happened."

"Thank you, sir," Jaxon said, reaching to shake his hand.

It didn't matter. He had a question and it had been answered.

Pete and Sadia stormed the track along with others he didn't know. Sadia flung her arms around him, squeezing him tight.

"You were amazing!" she shrilled.

"Dude, where have you been hiding all that speed?" Pete asked.

We are a lot faster than that.

Other people flocked around them and started snapping pictures.

"How did it feel to beat the fastest man alive?" a woman asked, thrusting a microphone in his face.

We beat the second fastest man alive, the *inner* voice whispered, full of pride. *We are the fastest.*

"It was a thrill and an honor to be here," Jaxon said,

struggling to not echo his *inner* voice.

He turned to Pete.

"Let's get out of here."

"Why? You're going to be famous," Pete said, grinning broadly.

Jaxon didn't want to be famous. Well, not that he had an objection to it, but that wasn't the point. He didn't run the race to be famous. He ran it for a much more personal reason. It was his first step to understanding who he really was and what he was becoming.

There's so much more we can do.

"I think he's right," Sadia murmured, looking at all the reporters. "It's gotten a bit crowded."

"Just a reminder, ladies and gentlemen, the Olympic trials will start in twenty minutes," the announcer said. "Make sure to stick around and root for your favorites."

Jaxon, Sadia, and Pete quickly headed off the track.

"I thought for sure that one guy who collapsed was

going to fall right into your lane and knock you over,"
Pete said.

Jaxon frowned, the memory of that was slowly coming back to him. "What happened to that guy?"

"Heat man! It's like a bazillion degrees out here."

"102 to be exact," Sadia corrected.

"Same diff. I don't know why you or anyone would want to be running on a day like this. It's too hot to live let alone move."

"Aren't you the one always complaining about being cold?" Sadia asked.

"Not ever again after today," Pete said.

Jaxon chuckled.

"Besides, me and my boy here are going to burn to a crisp in this sun," Pete said.

Sadia rolled her eyes. "Boys, always complaining about a bit of sun."

They made it to the car and as they were climbing in,

Jaxon inadvertently glanced at the side mirror. Instead of seeing a lanky eighteen-year-old kid with pale skin and brown hair he saw the *inner*, the voice that whispered from inside. The image reflected back to him looked more focused, more mature in some way. He was well-muscled and had the look of a stalking panther. He was bronze with brown intense eyes that seemed to bore right through Jaxon's soul. His mirror image smirked.

Ready for the next challenge?

Jaxon so much wanted to answer, he wanted to ask him why this sudden need to prove himself, themselves, whatever they were. He didn't dare while Pete and Sadia were there, though. Neither of them knew about the *inner*. He wanted to keep it that way.

"Dude, stop admiring yourself already," Pete said. "Get in the car. I needs my AC!"

* * *

"I still can't believe you didn't want to stick around and bask in all the glory," Pete said as they were driving out of The City of Angels, heading north for Yerba Buena.

"I for one think it really showed great character," Sadia said. "You're amazing and humble."

That wasn't it, but he wasn't ready yet to explain to either of them what he wanted. What he needed.

"Yeah, but humble doesn't pay the bills. I bet if you'd stuck around you could have gotten a spot on the Olympic team," Pete said.

"What would've been the point? I've already beaten the best."

"The point? Um... the great honor of representing our country, worldwide fame, sponsorships? Someone needs to make money off your skills."

"Someone already did make money off them," Sadia

said pertly.

"What are you talking about?" Jaxon asked.

"I made a slight wager with a gentleman in the stands," Pete said. "He gave me 20-1 odds."

"How much did you make?"

"Five thousand dollars. Hey, half of it's yours if you want it."

"No, thanks," Jaxon said absently as he stared out the window at the scenery flashing by.

"Well, I'll keep a separate stash just for you," said Pete.

* * *

June 16, 2018br around sunset

Yerba Buena

Jaxon was standing in a small courtyard surrounded by

tropical trees and plants. Behind the building in front of him, mountains painted the distant sky. A stiff breeze brought with it the smell of the ocean that was close by.

His eyes were focused on a man in his thirties, dressed in an all-white silk Yi-fu. He had a slim build with an incredibly calm and focused demeanor. He and Jaxon had just exchanged a few brief words and were now facing off, preparing to fight.

That wasn't even the odd part. They were speaking to each other in Mandarin. Jaxon never learned Mandarin and yet the words poured out of him. He knew the other man responded in kind and yet, somehow, he'd understood him.

He was facing down one of the greatest martial arts masters of all time, Master Marshall Lee. Jaxon himself had taken exactly eight kung-fu lessons when he was seven.

A small group gathered to watch comprised mostly

of Master Lee's students. Sadia and Pete stood with them. Pete was sporting a brand new sunburn and was doing his best to smile at a couple of cute girls as though there was nothing in the world wrong with him. To the girls it was obvious he was in pain, as they kept giggling and talking behind their hands to one another.

Master Lee bowed and Jaxon bowed back. Jaxon cleared his mind, and at the moment the only thing he did remember was his handful of lessons.

Lee leaped at him, moving so swiftly that Jaxon barely could see his attack. He felt the impact, though, on his stomach and chest. Pain flared up, hot and intense, and he grunted.

Let go!

Lee stepped back, giving him a second to catch his breath. Once he recovered, Jaxon sprung forward with a kick. With his left hand Lee deflected his foot and followed with a counter right then turned away effortlessly. Jaxon found himself crouched over on the ground, with the wind knocked out of him.

Let go and let me do this!

Jaxon was in full agreement. Before he could relinquish control, he felt it wrestled from him. In a flash he realized somehow he was back on his feet, with no memory of having stood up. He turned to face his opponent.

The master leapt forward with a side high kick. Where his moves before seemed lightning fast now it felt like Jaxon was watching them in slow motion. He could see the delicate movement of Master Lee's fabric. He could see each individual hair on his opponent's head. He could almost feel what techniques his opponent was planning to use next.

Jaxon casually side stepped the kick and blocked. He returned a right and a left, the master blocked both. Lee returned a left and a right, mirroring his opponent's moves. Jaxon blocked both. It was as if Jaxon was actually learning how to fight, while fighting. The master, confident in his Wing Chun style, arrogantly brushed his nose with his left thumb and threw a surprise right hand. Jaxon sidestepped it and caught him flush with a powerful right to the stomach.

The master fell to the ground. He quickly returned to his feet, but it was clear Jaxon's move caught him off guard, and he was in pain.

The master eyed him warily and went into a defensive stance. Jaxon realized that all the pain from the first volley he withstood earlier in the fight was gone. All he felt was the growing power of the *inner* force in his veins, and he marveled at the prospect of proving what he could do with it.

He advanced with a roundhouse, then a hook kick into a spinning hook kick at a lighting speed. Jaxon had no intention of landing any of them, he was clearly toying with Master Lee, as he continued to back up in full defensive mode. Jaxon attempted a punch into a side kick. At the last second Lee blocked them both.

The master took another step back as Jaxon launched a back kick. He was aiming to kick the master in the face. Lee quickly sidestepped and Jaxon only grazed him.

"Where did you train?" Lee asked him in Mandarin. attempting to stall and give himself time to recover from Jaxon's assaults.

"Wo meiyou xunlian," Jaxon said, admitting he hadn't trained anywhere.

"Impossible," Lee said.

"I'm learning as we fight, so you're actually my teacher," said Jaxon.

He leaped forward with a kick to the Master's solar-plex. Lee's hand only partially blocked it this time, and Jaxon landed a glancing blow with his left hand.

The Master tried to strike back but Jaxon easily sidestepped out of reach, not even bothering to block the flurry of attacks. He just effortlessly dodged every punch and kick.

"There's something different about you," Lee said.

"Much different?" Jaxon responded.

Jaxon launched another assault. This time he landed three solid blows to the face, chest, and stomach.

While falling back the Master grabbed Jaxon's right arm after the last blow, in an attempt to gain leverage to throw. Jaxon recognized the Master's attempt and countered it with an inside slip move into a hip toss, and threw the Master to the ground. Jaxon sprung instantly into a drop kick toward his head.

The Master gasped as he snapped his own head back to avoid taking the brunt of the kick. Jaxon's toes grazed his chin.

Before he could stand Jaxon closed the distance and

began raining a flurry of blows on the Master's shoulders, neck, and back. The master went to one knee in defense, waiting for an opening.

Jaxon's blink was all he needed. Caught off guard, Lee took the opportunity to strike him, sending him back just far enough so that Lee could leap to his feet.

Suddenly Jaxon felt as if he was exploding. Energy like molten fire poured through his veins. He lurched forward, unable to visually track the speed at which his hands were moving. As Jaxon leapt forward, punching, kicking repeatedly, Lee continued backpedaling under the ferocity of the onslaught. Moving so fast he could barely see what he was doing as hands and feet lashed out, kicking, striking. He felt the impacts, but only faintly, he knew he was landing hard attacks with stopping power.

Finally, at point blank range, Jaxon landed a powerful one inch punch on the Master's chin. His head snapped back, his eyes rolled over white, he fell to the ground and laid motionless.

Jaxon stood, calm as the adrenalin left his system. He could see the rise and fall of Master Lee's chest.

Don't worry, I didn't put everything on that punch because we could've killed him, the *inner* said. *But he'll definitely feel that for a few days.*

Jaxon took several steps backward as Lee's students crowded around him. He looked down at his hands. There wasn't a mark on them. They weren't even red where they'd been striking Master Lee. He realized during the whole encounter he never broke a sweat or started breathing hard.

Child's play.

He glanced up in time to see Pete and Sadia coming toward him.

Jaxon couldn't help but wonder what was next.

* * *

31

June 19, 2018br

Yerba Buena

"What's wrong?" Sadia asked.

"Nothing" Jaxon responded.

"We've been in Yerba Buena for three whole days and seen some cool stuff, but you seem like you're somewhere else."

"No, I'm good, I'm here," he said.

"I don't-"

Both their phones pinged. Jaxon quickly pulled his out of his pocket and read the text message. It was from Pete.

Meet me at Ripley's in 20 min.

"Pete wants us to meet him at Ripley's Believe It or Not in twenty minutes," he said.

"Why?" Sadia asked.

Why? Jaxon texted back.

It's a surprise!

For who? Jaxon texted

For you! Get down here!

What about lunch? Jaxon responded

It can wait until after. *Srsly. U will love this.*

"What's going on?" Jaxon asked as Pete hurried up to them a few minutes later, grinning like an idiot.

"You'll see," Pete said, grabbing Jaxon's arm and pulling him toward a man.

"Here we are," Pete said proudly.

The man turned to look at him. "Great, just in time. Now where is this superhuman strongman?"

"Right here, Mr. Harrington," Pete said, clapping Jaxon on the shoulder.

Mr. Harrington looked Jaxon over with a perplexed look then turned back to Pete.

"You're kidding, right?"

"No, I'm not. He's a lot stronger than he looks."

"Kid, I don't have time for pranks."

"It's not, honest!" Pete said.

"What's going on?" Jaxon asked.

"What's going on, young man, is that we're doing a live event today with the world's strongest man. Your friend here convinced me that he knew someone who could give Buford a run for his money and that it would be good publicity. I agreed to give you a chance to arm wrestle Buford."

A surge of excitement swept through Jaxon.

Yes, yes, we can do it!

"We can do it! I mean, I can do it," Jaxon said eagerly.

"I'm afraid not young man, you just aren't as advertised."

The statue.

Jaxon turned and looked at a statue of what looked like an elephant man nearby.

"How much does that statue way?" he asked.

"Several hundred pounds. Why?" Mr. Harrington asked.

Jaxon walked over, his heart pounding in his chest. He wrapped his arms around it.

"What are you doing?" Mr. Harrington asked

Relax, we can do this.

Jaxon hefted it in the air over a foot off the ground and gently put it back down. Part of him couldn't believe what he just done, but another part of him was always ready, hungry for something more challenging. He turned and saw Mr. Harrington gaping at him. The man slowly nodded up and down.

"Okay, you've got your chance."

* * *

Buford turned out to be a giant of a man, almost seven feet tall and with arms that were each bigger than Jaxon's waist.

"This is awesome!" Pete said, so excited that his voice went high and squeaky.

"This is crazy," Sadia said, staring wide-eyed at Buford.

"He looks like he could rip your arm off!"

"Sure" Pete said, "but this isn't an arm ripping contest so we've got this made!"

"We?" Jaxon asked.

Pete grabbed Jaxon by the shoulders and gave him a quick, rough massage.

"And by 'We' I mean you, and your fantastically gorgeous cheerleader, and your financial advisor."

"As I remember you always got D's in math," Jaxon said.

"But at multiplication I'm a whiz." Pete replied.

"Multiplication?" Jaxon asked, raising an eyebrow.

Sadia rolled her eyes.

"He means he placed more bets on you."

"Only modest ones," Pete said. "At the odds I was getting, who wouldn't?"

"Nice to know you have so much faith in me," said Jaxon

"Look, you told me you could beat Reggie Rapid, and Mater Lee and I thought you were crazy, but you did. You always bet on your friends, right? Now you tell me you can beat the steroid king over there-"

"Actually, I believe you were the one who said that," Jaxon interrupted.

"You, me, we've known each other so long that those words aren't really applicable. You know, it's us. Me-us said you could beat him. You-us agreed to do so. Me-us believes you."

"And which 'us' collects the bet money?" Jaxon asked.

"That would be Me-us."

Sadia cleared her throat.

Pete sighed.

"And then Me-us gives it to Her-us to hold onto because Her-us is more responsible than any of us."

"And don't you forget it," Sadia said with a smile. She stepped closer to Jaxon and looked up at him with wide, brown eyes.

"You okay?" she asked softly.

"Yeah, I'm fine," Jaxon reassured her.

"You don't have to do this if you don't want to. That's your official cheerleader speaking."

Yes we do, the *inner* voice insisted.

"I know," Jaxon said tightly.

"Do or do not. There is no try," Pete interjected, doing his best Yoda impression.

Sadia glanced over her shoulder, giving Pete a glare.

"Ladies and gentlemen, thank you for coming out to see this extraordinary event!" Mr. Harrington was on his microphone and was addressing the crowd.

This is going to be fun, the *inner* voice said, drowning out whatever introductions Mr. Harrington was making.

Moments later Buford stepped over the velvet rope and seated himself at one of the chairs at the table. Jaxon slowly sat down in the chair opposite of his opponent. Buford stared at him for a moment and then burst out laughing.

"Okay, I thought you were joking. Funny. Who is this guy and where's this mighty Jaxon I'm supposed to arm wrestle?" Buford asked.

"That's me," Jaxon said quietly.

Jaxon took a deep breath. He put his right elbow on the pad, with his right hand up, ready to lock up. He grabbed the stabilizer bar with his left hand. Buford

looked at Mr. Harrington who must've nodded because

the big man turned back to Jaxon.

"Boy, someone needs to learn you to respect your

betters and not bite off more than you can chew," Buford

growled.

When he slammed his elbow down on the table the

whole thing shook. Jaxon refused to blink even though

he could feel tendrils of anxiety flaring up in the pit of

his stomach. Buford wrapped his huge hand around

Jaxon's. In the big man's grip Jaxon's hand looked like

that of a child. He could see the muscles in Buford's arm

flexing, tensing.

Don't worry, I've got this. Let me take care of him.

Jaxon hoped the *inner* knew what it was doing, even

though he did want to try his hand first. Buford squeezed

his hand tightly. Jaxon felt the bones in his hand

grinding against each other.

He's trying to intimidate us.

Mr. Harrington placed his hand over the top of Buford's and Jaxon's.

"Back your shoulder up, close your hands. Go!" Mr. Harrington suddenly released them. Buford moved like a cobra and within a moment Jaxon's hand was hovering less than an inch above the pad. Thinking strategically Jaxon decided to break contact.

Let go and let me do this, this is about strategy, not just power.

Jaxon closed his eyes for a moment and let go of control. He felt a surge of power rush through his arm. With his renewed confidence he opened his eyes.

After breaking contact Mr. Harrington was forced to use the straps. Immediately after strapping them together and checking their elbows and shoulders Mr. Harrington said, "Go!" and released them.

We are going to take him into deep waters, then

drown him.

Buford struck fast again, but his force was halted as if he'd hit a brick wall. Buford was staring at him with a look of shock on his face as Jaxon steadily raised their hands back to the start position.

We just need to stay steady a little longer.

There were a few moments of stasis, where Buford was straining to make any headway against Jaxon. Then Jaxon felt a surge of energy run through him. The muscles in his arm pulsed and he suddenly moved Buford's arm. He could barely feel any resistance from him. Sweat popped out on Buford's brow and then Jaxon slammed his hand down onto the table with such force that the table broke in half.

Buford screamed in agony and surged to his feet. His hand was bleeding profusely where it made contact with the table. He staggered back, popped the hand straps, got tangled in the velvet rope, and fell backward, hitting the ground with a thud.

The bigger they are, the harder they fall, the *inner* voice chortled.

The crowd was going wild. Harrington thrust the microphone directly into Jaxon's face.

"What do you have to say to the world?" the man practically screamed in excitement.

"The bigger they are, the harder they fall," Jaxon said.

Now you're getting it. We're unstoppable. And we're going to prove it.

* * *

At Jaxon's insistence they left Yerba Buena that afternoon. Mr. Harrington tried to convince Jaxon to do a display for the museum as the world's strongest man. That wasn't a part of Jaxon's mission. He just wanted to get out of there and find the next challenge.

What's next to conquer?

Jaxon sat in the backseat, contemplating everything that happened while Sadia and Pete chatted excitedly up front.

"How much did you make?" Jaxon finally asked.

"Well, I placed several bets this time and I cleaned up, ten-thousand dollars. I'm rich!"

"No, but you will be," Jaxon said.

"What do you mean?" Pete asked.

"I mean, why stop now?"

Sadia twisted around in the seat to look at him. Her eyes were wide.

"What on earth are you thinking about?" she asked.

He cleared his throat. "I'm wondering what else I can do."

"Haven't you done enough? You proved you're the fastest man in the world, the best fighter, and the strongest. What more is there?" she asked.

"Hand-eye coordination," Pete spoke up for him.

"What?"

"You know, can he outshoot the best basketball player, outthrow the best quarterback?"

"Oh yeah, and I'm sure they're all going to agree to be challenged by an 18-year-old they've never heard of," Sadia said.

"Why not?" Jaxon asked.

"Yeah, and thanks to me posting on Burbngram, Jaxon isn't exactly unheard of anymore," Pete piped up.

"I don't like this," Sadia said, frowning.

"What? You don't like me beating the best at everything?" Jaxon asked.

"It's not that. I just don't understand. I mean, you saw that guy, how did you beat him?"

Jaxon said, "I found… *inner* strength."

"Inner strength?" Sadia asked, raising an eyebrow

skeptically.

"Yeah."

"That's not what inner strength is," Sadia said.

Pete piped up.

"Self-actualization, seeing the goal in his mind and making it happen, law of attraction, all that stuff."

"Yeah, but-"

"Who cares how he's doing it? What's important is that he is and he's on a roll. We need to take advantage of that before Dr. Banner back there stops being able to Hulk out at will."

"Maybe it's not natural, but it is happening. And I, for one, need to see how far this goes," Jaxon said.

"Me, two!" Pete said.

"I don't understand the path you're on," Sadia said.

"Neither do I." He hesitated. "Just because we can't see where it leads, does that mean you don't want to walk it with me?"

Sadia dropped her eyes.

"Of course, I want to walk it with you. This path or any other path you might find," she said, her voice soft, almost yearning.

"Then let's not worry until there's something to worry about," he said.

"We're with you, Jax, to the end," Pete said.

* * *

July 6, 2018br

Lenape (Delaware Nation)

RCA Dome

Thanks to Pete's Burbngram pics Jaxon's celebrity status was rapidly growing. It was odd that people were starting to recognize him. It'd been three weeks since he outraced Reggie Rapid and every day seemed to add to his legion of admirers.

Jaxon stepped onto the field and his eyes locked onto his friends. They were standing with the famous quarterback William Manning who was busy signing a football Pete brought for the occasion. In the stands were a sizable group of people including what looked like a handful of reporters.

Jaxon strode forward, barely hearing the cheers of those who were waiting to see the exhibition to come. He reached the small group of people and extended his hand. "Mr. Manning, it is an honor."

William shook his hand warmly. "It's not every day I get to meet an Arpanet legend," he said with a chuckle.

"And it's not every day that I get to meet the world's greatest quarterback," Jaxon replied.

"Shall we?" William asked.

Jaxon nodded.

They were standing on the fifty-yard line. In the

endzone was the target, a moving net floating from sideline to sideline.

"Good luck," Sadia said with a quick smile before she hauled Pete off the field.

As soon as they made it to the sideline, William picked up one of footballs that was in the basket.

"You need to warm up?" he asked.

Jaxon shook his head no. "You?"

"Already did."

William turned slightly so his left side was facing the endzone. He cocked back his arm, sighted, and threw the ball in a tight spiral all the way down the field. It hit the moving target squarely in the net. The crowd roared. William stepped back, with a look of satisfaction on his face.

Jaxon bent down and picked up a ball. He hadn't thrown one in a long time. Still, it felt comfortable as he wrapped his hand around it.

Give me the reins.

He nodded, relaxing his body and mind.

He turned his left side toward the endzone. He cocked back his arm, sighting down the field. When it released it flew from his fingers with the slightest wobble, but it made it all the way to its destination, hitting the target in the net just as William's did.

Then he and Manning both backed up ten yards to the second throwing location. Manning rapidly threw two balls back to back, both hitting the moving target right in the net.

Quicker than thought, Jaxon grabbed his balls, stood up and threw each without hesitation. The first ball left his hand in a perfect spiral, so did the second. It was the best he'd ever thrown, and they sailed downfield, again hitting the net right on target.

"Nice job, kid! You thinking of going pro?" Manning asked.

"No, sir," Jaxon said.

They backed up ten more yards. Manning looked more serious as he slowly picked up the ball. Seventy yards. It seemed impossibly long.

The moment Manning let the ball fly Jaxon knew it was going to land low. It did, dropping quickly toward the end and hitting the moving target below the net and bouncing up in the air. Manning shook his head.

Jaxon picked up the ball and again let it fly almost in a single motion. The ball rocketed from his fingertips. It sailed down the field and again hit the target perfectly in the center of the net.

"Dang, kid, you're good," Manning muttered. "Congratulations."

"Thanks," Jaxon said. "Want to go further back?"

Manning shook his head. "There's a handful that might get close to eighty yards, but I know when I'm licked."

Disappointment surged through Jaxon even as he reached out to shake the hand that Manning offered to him.

We're not done, the *inner* voice said.

Jaxon turned abruptly, feeling like he lost complete control of his own movements. He walked another ten yards, picked up the football, and kept walking until he reached the far endzone. He turned. One-hundred yards separated him from the moving target. No quarterback had ever done it.

When Jaxon threw the ball it left his hand at ferocious speed. There was barely any arc to it. On the far side of the field it struck the target dead center with so much force it went right through the net and hit the back wall of the endzone.

People in the stands leapt to their feet.

"That was amazing!" Pete gushed a minute later when he ran up to him.

"How much did you win?" Jaxon asked.

Pete shook his head slowly. "I didn't bet."

"What? Why not?" Jaxon asked.

"Dude, it was William Manning. I couldn't bet against my hero. You get it, right?" Pete asked, as his voice was imploring.

"I can't believe you passed up the opportunity to make more money."

"Fortunately, I didn't," Sadia smiled. She opened her purse and Jaxon could see that it was stuffed full of money.

"Whoa, how much did you make?" Pete asked.

"Let's just say… a lot. Anyone want to take a little side trip to The Kingdom of Hawaii?" she asked.

"Yes! Beaches, luaus, and bikini clad babes! Count me in!" Pete said enthusiastically. "And while I'm dancing with some hula hottie, our boy here can win the Iron Man."

"Actually, we had something a bit different in mind,"
Jaxon said thoughtfully.

"We? We who?" Sadia asked, frowning.

"I mean, me. I. I have something different in mind,"
he amended hastily.

* * *

July 17th, 2018br

The Norwegian man sitting across the table from
Jaxon was studying the chess board between them with
the practiced eye of a grand master. Stephen Carlsen was
actually the top-rated chess player in the world. And he
was about to lose.

"Checkmate," Jaxon said as he moved his Queen.

Stephen stared at the board for a moment, muttered
something in his mother tongue, then tipped over his

king.

Jaxon sat back, blinking. He'd done it! He won!

We won. We won.

He stood up, shook his opponent's hand, and walked off stage. Sadia threw her arms around his neck and planted a kiss on his cheek.

"You did it!" she shrieked. "You did it, you did it, you did it!"

"Yes," he said, staring at her as he tried to gather his thoughts.

"Now can we go to a beach?" Pete asked.

"Or home! let's talk about it over dinner, I'm starving," Sadia said, taking Jaxon's arm and leading him toward the exit.

Concentrating on it. With my eyes closed, I can focus on the feeling. It's still just a vibration, tiny but building. Something about this change gives me pause. I know, but I don't understand what this occurrence is. The energies are aligned along a different axis, but I cannot see a pattern. I cannot decipher its source. How can anyone comprehend this? It is coming! No matter the force at play, I will remain open and receive it with my usual equanimity. Time offers many opportunities to practice reacting properly. Patience, calm, steadiness – these are my gifts.

Whatever this is … it's different. I can feel its echoes and ripples without being able to see any of it. It's perhaps the biggest disruption to the mundane I've encountered, but ultimately a disturbance is a disturbance.

I inhale time and hold it in my lungs, safe. Trying to keep the world from self-destruction, to guard life from demolition, it can be exhausting. There always seems to be some entity trying to take. Take power, take control, take what isn't theirs. It's an eternal battle that plays out within seconds. I'm prepared for whatever is to come, and I know it isn't prepared for me. My age and experience have taught me more than others can learn in a hundred lifetimes, yet this force is juvenile, drunk on its ability to destroy. Like a tornado grown too powerful to stay on course, it is unraveling with ever greater speed, but I can see the collision coming. I can brace for it.

I exhale second by second, considering what it will take to do battle with this element. What is the plane of war? What is the end he means? My brow furrows as I once again zero in on the sensation of dissonance. I wonder who else is aware.

Chapter 2

Seeking

July 20, 2018br

District of Columbia

Jaxon got out of the car and waved to Pete and Sadia before turning toward his front door. They were gone a little over a month on their road trip and now he was back home. Somehow, the two-story house he grew up in seemed a lot smaller than it did before he left. It was changed somehow. He was also changed.

It was true. He wasn't the same guy that left this house in search of…something. Out there he found himself. Well, at least part of himself. Unfortunately, in the finding, he ended up with more questions about who and what he was.

His *inner* self was very clear on the fact that he hadn't finished testing his limits yet.

We've only just begun, his *inner* self said.

For the last week Jaxon hadn't been able to see anything of his physical body when he looked in a mirror. All he saw was the *inner* self. He started to panic until he realized no one else could see the reflection he saw.

He headed up the front stairs and opened the front door.

"Mom, Dad, I'm home!" he called out.

"Jaxon!" he heard his mother call.

A moment later she ran into the room and threw her

arms around him in a bear hug. Jenna Randle was a beautiful woman. Since he was ten, half his classmates had a crush on her. There was something magnetic about her smile which lit up any room she was in.

"Your father's not home from work yet," she said.

She brushed a strand of hair out of his eyes.

"Someone needs a haircut," she laughed.

He smiled. "Yeah, it is getting a little long. I missed you."

"Not half as much as I missed you," she said, ruffling his hair.

"Prove it," he replied. It was a long-standing joke between them.

"I made your favorite lasagna for dinner and I'm baking chocolate chip cookies."

"You did miss me!"

"Why don't you drop your laundry off in the washroom and get cleaned up. Your father will be home in about an hour and then we'll eat."

"Sounds good," he said. He gave her a quick kiss on the cheek and then headed for the stairs.

* * *

Twenty minutes later he stepped out of the bathroom, with only a towel wrapped around his waist. There was nothing like a hot shower to make you feel refreshed.

He turned on his computer and listened as it woke up and went through its routine. There was an odd, high-pitched sound he didn't remember hearing before.

As he put on some clean clothes, he tried to block out the sound. It just kept going, though. He tried restarting but the sound returned even louder.

"What is wrong with you?" he muttered.

He crouched down to take a look at the CPU and blew some dust off of the air vents. He got up and went to get a screwdriver. He came back, sat down on the floor, and moments later removed the outer case. He stared at the inner workings of his computer with no clue as to what he was looking for. He could do some stuff with software and he'd taken one quarter of programming at school, but he knew virtually nothing about hardware.

Let's take a look at it.

"You're seeing it. You see what I see," he said jokingly.

I think I see the problem, let me take over.

"Ok, let's fix it."

Jaxon watched as his hands began to fly. He grabbed the motherboard and began yanking wires. Part of him was aghast at what he was doing, but the *inner* self seemed confident. His hands worked feverishly fast as he moved, tweaked, rewired.

"Hey, son, welcome home!"

Jaxon looked up, dazed, as his father, Julius, entered the room.

Julius stopped short, eyes going wide.

"What on earth happened to your computer?"

Jaxon looked back down and realized that there were parts scattered all over the floor in a semicircle around him. He was holding something in his hand that he didn't even know the name of much less what it did or where it went. If this looked crazy to him he could only imagine what it looked like to his father. He struggled to find the words to explain to him what he was doing.

We're fixing it.

"I'm fixing it," Jaxon said out loud.

"By.... breaking it?"

It wasn't right.

"It…it wasn't working."

"Okay, but when did you learn to fix computers?"

He waited a moment for the *inner* voice to say

something, but it remained silent. He realized that his father was waiting for an answer.

Jaxon grimaced. "I took an online course a while back."

"Oh, wow. Good for you. You know, I've got a dead USB port on the computer in my office. Maybe you could take a look at it."

"Sure, Dad."

"Well, I don't want to interrupt you, but your mother said dinner will be ready in ten minutes."

"Okay, thanks."

"It's good to have you home."

"Thanks, Dad. Missed you."

"You, too," his father said before taking another sweeping glance at the parts scattered all over the floor. He shook his head slightly before leaving the room. As soon as he was gone Jaxon sagged in relief. He was going to have to start coming up with answers because people were going to start asking a lot more questions.

He needed to know what to say, how to explain to them.

We don't need to explain ourselves.

"Great."

Jaxon turned back to the mess on the floor. He'd heard that the secret to taking things apart and putting them back together again was to do so in a precise order, so that you could just reverse the process. Looking at the mess, though, he couldn't make out any order in the chaos. He was certain that the parts were just scattered around haphazardly.

"I hope you know what you're doing," he muttered.

I got this.

* * *

Dinner was odd just because it was so normal. Jaxon was grateful, but also a little sad. He would've liked to brag about his accomplishments and have them ooh and aah over them, but he knew that would bring with it questions he didn't have the answers to.

They did ask him what all he saw and did. He gave them an abbreviated version of events, not sure they could handle the full truth. The lasagna was good, but he could tell that his mom left it in the oven probably about three minutes too long. When she brought out the chocolate chip cookies he discovered that he could taste every single ingredient in them, and some parts of it gave off the weirdest chemical taste.

"How are the cookies?" his mom asked.

"Delicious," he said, privately wondering how he was going to convince her of that if he could barely force himself to choke down one. He didn't understand. Chocolate chip cookies were his favorite.

"Did you do anything different with these, Mom?" he asked.

"Not a thing. The same recipe I've been making since I was younger than you," she said with a smile.

The cookie tastes that old, the *inner* voice said sarcastically.

Jaxon smiled and grabbed another. Once he ate it, he carried the plates into the kitchen and loaded the dishwasher. He put the leftovers in the refrigerator and then grabbed the garbage and hauled it outside.

The sky was a brilliant sapphire blue without a cloud in it. He stared up at it, but instead of just admiring the color or the clearness of the evening, he found himself thinking about the science behind the color saturation. He shook his head and went back inside, determined to get upstairs, hopefully put his computer back together, and start working on figuring out what was happening to it.

"Thanks, Mom, it was all delicious," he said in what he hoped was a convincing tone as he walked back by the dining room.

"Only the best for my boy," she said with a grin.

Only the best....

"And in the morning, I'm making waffles," she added.

"I can't wait," he said forcefully hoping that they would taste like they should and that whatever was happening with his tastebuds would calm down by then. With all the other problems he was having, a sudden aversion to food was the last thing he wanted to have to deal with, let alone explain.

Jaxon quickly made his way back upstairs where his computer was still in pieces. None of it made any sense as he surveyed the damage. It looked like he ripped every single part of the thing apart. He sat down in the middle of it with a heavy sigh.

"You know, I wanted to surf the arpanet tonight before going to bed."

Don't worry, we will.

"I don't see how."

You will.

"Alright, it's your show."

Ten minutes later he found himself screwing the case back into place. He reached for the power button and winced slightly.

"Here goes nothing."

At first he thought nothing happened because there was silence. Then he saw lights starting to blink. Suddenly his screen flickered to life with his login page.

"Whoa, that was fast and super quiet."

Not only was the high-pitched whine gone but all the other startup sounds were gone as well.

"Unbelievable," he muttered.

Wait for it.

He got up and sat down in his chair then rolled himself up to the keyboard. Moments later he was online and every page loaded with blinding speed.

"How did you do that? I saw it, my hands fixed it, but I still don't believe it."

I could explain it, but you wouldn't understand.

"Ha ha."

Time to take things to the next level. Time to test our mental capacity, push our limits.

"I thought that was what the chess match was about."

That was just the warm-up. It's time to run the mental race.

Before Jaxon could say anything his fingers began flying over the keys. He'd never typed so fast in his life. A second later he was clicking on a website which detailed that a pharmaceutical company recently made a huge breakthrough in quantum medicine. It was fascinating reading. As he progressed he could feel something happening in his brain.

It was like a series of small, electrical shocks like his

braincells were all suddenly firing rapidly. There were dozens of them, some firing together, others staggered. He jerked and twitched but kept his eyes glued to the screen. In seconds he came to the end of the report and was shocked to see that it was nearly a hundred pages long.

"That's impossible," he whispered.

Impossible is only something we haven't achieved yet.

"What's next?"

What isn't?

* * *

Jaxon's fingers felt like they were on fire. He pulled them off the keyboard and realized that the tips looked almost blistered. Crazier still, the keyboard was giving off heat. He'd split his screen in two so he could read two documents at the same time. When he first started reading he was researching myths and legends, like the labors of Hercules. He'd found myths and legends across numerous cultures about the feats of gods and demigods.

His junior year history teacher always said that if you looked hard enough, you could usually find a grain of truth in all myths and legends. He was staring at two different texts, one was two thousand years old and the other twice that. One was written in Mandarin and the other in Cuneiform.

He'd been reading through them at lightning speed before his fingers had gotten so hot. Now, sitting there staring at both texts, he realized two things. First, they shared a lot in common. The tone and word choice, even the topics, sounded like they were written by the same person. Second, the translators messed up about 5% of the Mandarin translation and 20% of the Cuneiform one.

He blinked rapidly, trying to understand what was

happening.

"Since when can we read either of these?"

We learned about five minutes ago.

It seemed impossible, but yet he could, and well enough that he knew when they were being mistranslated or the context was wrong.

"Unbelievable. How many languages do I know? Do we know?"

By the end of the night? All of them.

He shook his head. The fact was almost incomprehensible. He'd barely squeaked by in Spanish in high school.

Once he'd made note of what the Cuneiform text really said, it became even more eerily similar to the Mandarin one. He printed a page of each of the original texts out and then grabbed a pen. He went to town doing his own translation. The number "7" featured heavily in both although it seemed like that was the author referencing himself or a group in both cases.

"So weird."

He got up and went into the bathroom, shutting the door. He stared at his *inner* self in the mirror.

"Do you think it's possible they were written by the same person? Different continents, different cultures, two thousand years apart."

Yes! It is the same author. We need to find him.

Jaxon took a deep breath and look up directly into the reflection's eyes intensely.

"What makes you think he's still alive?"

The *inner* self looked at him, in deep thought slowly he nodded.

He is.

"How can we be sure?"

We'll have to find him.

"Is that even possible?"

There was a sudden knock on the bathroom door.

"Are you alright in there?" Jenna called. "Who are you talking to?"

He winced.

"Nobody, Mom. I was just talking to myself."

"Okay, Honey."

"What time is it?" he asked.

"It's one in the morning."

Jaxon stared at his *inner* self. He hadn't realized how much time had passed. His *inner* self didn't say anything.

"Thanks, Mom."

He heard her footsteps as she headed back to the master bedroom.

Jaxon splashed some water on his face and left the bathroom. Back in his room he eyed his bed. He should get some sleep, but in truth he wasn't tired.

We don't need sleep. We need information.

"Yeah, we do," he muttered under his breath.

The keyboard had cooled down considerably. When he looked at his fingers he noticed that the redness was gone, and his fingertips were healed completely. He sat down and began searching.

* * *

Half an hour later he had scoured tens of thousands of websites, and finally found what he was looking for. He started printing out more articles. One was a Cherokee text, another was Runic, the third was Hieroglyphic, and the fourth was Hindi. The fifth was the oldest of all and archaeologists apparently had not only been unable to translate it, but they also couldn't even figure out what civilization it came from. Part of the problem was it seemed to predate every other written language by at least twenty thousand years.

He was convinced that all five of them were written

by the same person who wrote the Cuneiform and Mandarin texts. Again, the number "7" appeared repeatedly. It was amazing.

He picked up his phone and called Sadia.

"Hello?" she answered groggily.

"Sadia, I've discovered the most amazing thing," he said.

"At two in the morning?"

"Yes. I've been up searching the arpanet super-fast. You should see it. Anyway, I found ancient texts from seven different cultures from all different time periods and they all read as if written by the same person."

"That's impossible," she said with a yawn.

"I know, but after I retranslated all of them into English, taking into account how syntax and grammar differ between the languages-"

"Jaxon, what are you talking about? You retranslated? What's going on?"

He sighed. "A lot. I'll tell you about it in the morning, okay?"

"Okay, goodnight."

"Goodnight," he said then hung up.

I don't think she will understand.

"I have to talk to somebody about this besides you."

* * *

Jaxon ended up getting a couple of hours of sleep. He woke up feeling refreshed. After breakfast, he video chatted with Sadia and Pete, both of whom were skeptical about what he was saying.

"Look, you guys just need to come over here. I can show you everything. Plus, there's a bunch of other stuff I'm starting to research. I'm beginning to think there's no limit to what I can figure out."

"Dude, I'd love to come see you tripping, but I'm

helping my folks pack for this three-day camping trip,"
Pete said. "I can come over tomorrow."

"Okay. Sadia?"

"Tomorrow works for me, too."

"Great. I'm going to keep doing what I'm doing so I
can show it to both of you tomorrow," Jaxon said,
struggling with his frustration and disappointment.

"We'll come over and you'll dazzle us with your
shiny new skills," Pete said. "And maybe afterward we
can hit the movies."

"That would be awesome," Sadia said.

"Sure," Jaxon said.

A minute later he hung up with them. They didn't
understand. There was nothing they could possibly see at
a movie theater that would compare with what he was
discovering right on his own computer.

He could tell that they were still very skeptical. That
was okay, he still had another day to gather more

evidence to show to them. Sadia was the head of the debate team in school. She would appreciate him backing up his arguments with facts and statistics.

We'll show them. We'll show the world.

* * *

July 23, 2018br

District of Columbia

That night Jaxon hacked into the most secure government databases in the world as he continued his search for information. It was no longer just about trying to track down the mysterious author. He was now absorbing every bit of knowledge he could from every different source.

Every scrap of scientific writing on science, health, math, the cosmos poured into his brain where he processed, catalogued, and indexed it. With each new discovery, his *inner* self grew more and more excited.

We're gaining true insight, growing in our awareness, I feel enlightened.

It was finally Friday morning. Jaxon was trying to finish up the research he was doing on time travel. He was hovering on the verge of a breakthrough. He'd managed to split his monitor so he could read four documents, then eight, then sixteen at once and he was racing through them, scarcely conscious of the actual words, but hurriedly absorbing them into his brain to sort through it all.

Suddenly, Jaxon could hear his friends talking outside. It seemed that all his senses had expanded and hearing was just the latest one that he was taking note of. His bedroom was at the front of the house and they must be outside the front door. He wasn't sure why they weren't just ringing the bell since they'd already arrived.

He stopped a moment to listen.

"Do I think he's gone mental? I don't know," Pete said.

"You have to admit that something weird is happening to him," Sadia said.

"Do I?"

"Come on, Pete."

"Look, all I know is that my best friend is going through some…changes."

"We're not talking about puberty," Sadia said sarcastically. "He's not growing facial hair and having his voice change. Everything is changing and he's becoming-"

"Superhuman?"

"Maybe not even human at all," Sadia said hesitantly, as though afraid to even voice the thought out loud.

"Oh, what, like's he's an alien or something and he's

managed to hide it from us our entire lives? Yeah, right."

"Maybe he doesn't even know what he is."

Jaxon got up and walked downstairs, continuing to listen as he did so.

"We have to be supportive."

"Yeah, but what does supportive look like? Playing into his delusions about whatever he thinks he found in those texts or maybe trying to get him some help?"

"Look, those crazy physical feats he did, those were all real, so just maybe we should hear him out. Maybe he's not as crazy as we're both worried he is."

"And if he is?"

Jaxon threw open the front door.

"You know I can hear you guys, right?" he asked.

He stopped.

His friends weren't on the porch. He could hear them, though, plain as day. He turned his head slowly and saw them sitting in Pete's car, which was parked across the street and halfway up the block.

His heart began to pound in his chest and the sound

of it was thunderous, drowning out whatever else his

friends were saying about him. He should go over to

them, but his feet didn't want to move. He'd heard

enough, and it didn't matter. What he was doing couldn't

be stopped, not even by his friends.

He turned and went back inside the house, leaving

the door unlocked. Inside his room he lifted his phone

off its charging pad. He texted Pete's phone.

Door's unlocked. Come up when u get here.

Moments later he got his friend's reply.

Just getting here. b up in a few.

That was fine. Jaxon sat back down at his computer.

He flexed his hands for a moment and then let them drop

onto the keyboard. Within moments he was immersed

yet again in the world of quantum physics. He read

through dozens of reports, articles, dissertations,

absorbing the information as he went.

A cough behind him startled him and his fingers stopped moving. He turned to see Pete and Sadia standing behind him, eyes wide and jaws hanging open.

"Oh, how long have you guys been standing there?" he asked.

"Two minutes," Pete said.

"I didn't know you were here," he said, deciding not to let them know he heard them talking in the car a few minutes earlier.

"Yeah, you texted me three minutes ago," Pete said.

"Were you really able to read all that?" Sadia asked. "The words were just streaming by, I couldn't make out any of it. You were typing and scrolling so fast…"

"Speed reading? Sure, it's easy," he said.

"That isn't like any speed reading I've ever seen," Sadia said.

Her pupils were dilated by two millimeters. Images

of her standing in his room at the same time of day at the same time of year flashed through his mind. They never dilated that much when adjusting to the light in his room.

She's afraid.

So was Pete. He could tell that by the change in his friend's body chemistry which produced a distinctive smell.

"So, what are you reading?" Pete asked.

"Right now, I'm just wrapping up quantum physics."

"You're wrapping it up?" Sadia asked wonderingly.

"Sure."

"Is that what you've been doing for two days?" Pete asked.

"Don't be ridiculous," Jaxon said, rolling his eyes.

Sadia and Pete both heaved sighs of relief.

"I've been studying just about everything: astrophysics, biochemistry, neuroscience, aerospace engineering, quantum mechanics, string theory, biomechanics engineering, nanotechnology, art, literature, and about a dozen languages."

"I see. And what exactly did you get out of all that in two days?" Sadia asked.

"What didn't I get out of it? I found cures for Aids, cancer, and the common cold. I hacked into some government computers and found all of Tesla's confiscated notebooks and figured out how to improve on his design for delivering free energy efficiently to the entire planet. I discovered that the math our researchers are using is antiquated and some of it flat out wrong. We look at gravity and flight in a completely messed up way. Time travel is not only possible, but is happening, we just aren't trained to interface with it just yet. I believe that if we got the right companies on board both time travel and teleportation can be affordable and widely available within five years. Of course, that opens us up to so many ethical questions, particularly about time travel. I've looked at how various philosophers would address the issue. I believe that Kant would say-"

"Whoa, Dude!" Pete said, throwing his hands up in the air. "We can't understand you. You started off speaking English and now…now I don't know what you're speaking. I heard like one phrase that I think was Latin."

"I speak three languages and that wasn't any of them," Sadia said.

Jaxon blinked. He focused on them.

"Can you understand me now?" he asked slowly.

"Yes. That. Was. In. English. Dude," Pete said.

Normally he may have gotten a bit irritated, but his head was just too full of information that was begging to be sifted through, calculated, and used. He sighed. He was going to have to go a lot slower with them than he would have liked. It was going to be tedious, but he needed to be able to share what he was learning with someone.

"Did you understand me when I said I came up with solutions to Aids, cancer, and the common cold? I've almost figured out aging as well. Just a little bit more research, and I think I'll be able to get it."

Pete chuckled. "Good joke. A cure to the common cold. Like doctors and scientists haven't been working on that one since the dawn of time."

"They have been, but they've been going about it all wrong. They've been trying to cure the body. Instead, you have to cure the mind and then let the mind cure the body."

Sadia was gaping at him.

"What?" he asked her.

"Are you serious?" she asked, her voice barely above a whisper.

"Completely"

"You…solved…three of the biggest health issues

that humanity faces in a day?"

He shrugged. "It was more like half a day. The majority of it was spent writing papers that I emailed to the various scientific, medical, and academic journals."

He waved his hand at a stack of bound reports nearly six inches thick that was sitting on one of his speakers. Sadia walked over to it, picked up the top report and began to flip through it.

"This is incredible," she muttered.

Pete walked over to her and started reading over her shoulder. After a minute he looked up at Jaxon.

"What the hell, man? We took all the same science classes in school. I've never seen most of these words and there's no way I could spell them let alone use them in a coherent sentence."

Jaxon shrugged. "I did all my research online. There's a wealth of knowledge out there if you can take the time to filter the good science from the junk and conspiracy theories. Of course, most of what we think of as scientific fact is destined to be thrown out in the next twenty years. Or even a few months if people bother to read my work."

"You had to copy this. You just printed out someone else's work and put your name on it," Pete said, growing more agitated.

"No, he didn't," Sadia said in an eerily calm voice.

"How do you know?"

"I've been proofreading essays for both of you since fifth grade. Jaxon's never once spelled the word 'because' right. He always spells it with a "bi", just like it is here."

"At least now I know why. It's the older spelling," he said. "That's the way we used to spell it."

"Who's 'we'?" Pete asked.

Jaxon frowned.

"English speakers. You know, us. Keep up."

Pete looked like he was going to say something else, but Sadia moved to another pile of papers, this one perched precariously on top of his backpack. She picked it up and stared at it for a moment. She slowly started shuffling through the different reports he'd written.

"A Treatise on Tesla and the Future of Free, Unlimited Energy. The Failings of Non-Euclidean Geometry in Light of the Movement of the Cosmos. The Creation of a Green Energy FTL Drive." She looked up. "You wrote all these?"

"That was yesterday afternoon," Jaxon said. "You should see the stack on the dresser."

She walked over and started thumbing through those.

"The Egyptian Discovery of the Americas. The Alphabet that Existed Before the Phoenicians. A Practical Guide to Fixing the American Jury System. The Socio-Political Landscape of the Next Thousand Years… this thing is 500 pages long!"

"Yeah, I think I started rambling a bit around the 2600s."

A single piece of paper fluttered onto the ground and she stooped down to pick it up. She glanced at it, then handed it to Pete whose eyes boggled.

"No way. Are you serious with this?" he asked, showing Jaxon the paper which was covered with Jaxon's scrawling handwriting.

"Yeah, I woke up at three in the morning and I knew how to make the definitive chocolate chip cookie. I decided I might as well write it down while I was at it."

"We need to go prove this theory right now," Pete said. "If this truly is the definitive chocolate chip cookie, then I'll believe all the rest of this," he said, waving his hands around the room.

"The cookie's not important," Jaxon said.

"Are you mental? Forget world peace or cold fusion or whatever else you've written down around here. This,

this right here could be the answer to the meaning of

life.”

Sadia sat down heavily on the edge of Jaxon’s bed

and just stared at him.

“What?” he finally asked.

“What’s happening to you?” she asked.

“I don’t know,” he admitted.

“How can you know literally everything else and not

know that?” she demanded.

“It’s…complicated,” he said with a sigh.

“Why are we still talking when we should be

baking?” Pete demanded, waving the piece of paper with

the cookie recipe in the air.

He can’t handle it. We’ve fried his brain.

Looking at Pete, Jaxon was concerned that it might

be true. He was just finding it harder to care. After all,

there was probably a cure for whatever was happening in

Pete’s brain right that minute. The right combination of

chemicals could balance out whatever was melting down. He could probably figure out how to make a smoothie for it if he raided the pantry and his parents' medicine cabinet.

"Can we all be serious for just five minutes?" Sadia asked.

"Who's not serious?" Pete asked. "Best cookies ever. Did you not hear that?"

It should have been funny, but it wasn't. That was because Pete wasn't joking. He was seriously having some sort of mental breakdown and he was clinging to the idea of the cookies because it was something tangible, relatable. He understood what cookies were and they were every day, mundane things. He could also imagine that one might come up with the recipe for the best cookie. That was as far as his brain was going to let him go at that moment, though.

I could have told you that they couldn't handle it.

"Okay, Pete, let's go bake some cookies."

* * *

Pete tried to eat half the cookie batter before Sadia wrested the bowl from him. She popped the first cookie sheet into the oven and glanced at Jaxon. "Hey, how much time are they in for?"

Time. He was submerged in deep thought meditating about time when they interrupted him upstairs. Time travel, backward, forward, so many numbers.

Something started to click in his mind. He sat down heavily in one of the chairs at the kitchen table. He closed his eyes for a moment, letting himself become lost in the sea of information that was swirling through his head. As if from a great distance he could hear Sadia talking to him. Her voice was rising in pitch, becoming more frantic. Pete grabbed his shoulders and shook him hard but he barely felt it. There was something he was reaching for. He almost had it. Whatever it was, it was important, perhaps the most important thing ever.

Come on, come on, the voice urged, impatience boiling over.

Jaxon was searching farther, faster, inside of his mind. He was scanning the universe of knowledge he absorbed earlier, looking for the thread that was eluding him. It was out there, the thing he wanted, needed to know. It felt like he was processing all the data the universe could supply him.

He could feel the blood rushing to his brain, leaving his extremities cold, almost lifeless. He could hear Sadia pleading, begging with him to wake up. She didn't understand, for most of his life he felt as if he was asleep and now he was finally awake.

Everything faded farther away, including Sadia and her sobs and Pete and his shouting. They didn't understand. They never would. They couldn't see the things he did, and could never see them either.

He was almost upon it, the little tiptoeing piece of information that was trying to hide itself from him. As if it could.

With a gasp he opened his eyes. Sadia and Pete both let go of him and jumped back, startled. He could see the fear on their strained faces. Sadia had been crying. He could smell the cookies burning in the oven.

"I know," he whispered.

Sadia and Pete exchanged anxious looks then turned back to him.

"What is it, buddy?" Pete asked, nervously licking his lips.

"What do you know?" Sadia asked breathlessly.

"I know the numbers."

What strange mist comes rolling in with the dawn? By my honor, no such mist has ever graced a morning before. Nay, not in the whole of history.

This, I suspect, is no average morning haze. While the sun creeps over the horizon in its predictable early movements, this foggy grey mist shines more radiant than any mere star.

Not the brilliance hewn from celestial jewels, those which fool weary souls into nighttime delusions. This fog comes in far too thick, too grey; a pungent soup-mist, too fiery for the tongue.

This misty, hazy star-smell overpowers my senses! The minute particles of my skin shift with its gravity. My muscles wither under its density. It towers over me like a mountain.

Though, let not fear hold back my search for truth, lest I be woe to bear a burden much greater. Neither death nor danger be worthy of my fear. Were that it manifested here before me, I would confront this power head-on!

Yet I sense that none of my powers would prevail against the strength of this novel mist that comes consuming the dawn.

Still, it must be said that not all grey skies bring rain. Such vast power has no need for the mundane evils of the tangible. This mist brings mysteries beyond the boundaries of this trifling world.

What might such a mist grow to become? The power it wields already, right now in its nascent state, is exploding from within my cells! What such power can exceed that of all the elements?

I must admit, it far exceeds my own.

No matter. If such a powerful being truly exists, I will not sit here and wait to be taken to slaughter like a lamb. If this mist be so mighty, I will fuel my own might to match.

Until the true nature of the behemoth reveals itself, my

sword will remain sharp.

Chapter 3

Winner's Circle

July 23, 2018br

District of Columbia

"What are you talking about?" Sadia asked.   "What numbers?"

Jaxon just stared up at her. "All of them."

Pete frowned. "What do you mean all of them?"

The smoke detector shrilled and Sadia ran over to turn off the oven. She pulled out a tray of burnt cookies and dropped them on top of the stove. She opened a window to vent the smoke and the detector finally stopped.

While she was working, Jaxon was busy going over everything that was flooding through his mind. Pete was just staring at him, still obviously agitated by whatever he thought was going on.

"What do you mean all of the numbers?" Pete asked.

"You name it. Statistics, probabilities, coordinates, everything."

"Give me an example."

Jaxon took a deep breath. How could he possibly explain to his friend everything that he was seeing? After all, it was like an entire universe of information had just exploded in his head and Pete…well Pete's head would just flat out explode if he tried to grasp it all.

"Ummm, how about…" he searched for something that would capture his friend's interest. "The winning lottery numbers?"

"You know the winning lottery numbers?" Pete asked, eyes bugging out of his head. "You mean, like the ones they drew last week?"

"No, like the ones they're going to draw today, tomorrow all of them."

Pete sat down hard in a chair.

"You're kidding me."

"38-24-7-13-47 and 2."

Pete leaned forward eagerly. "We've got to test your new powers!"

Yes, let's test ourselves, Jaxon's *inner* voice agreed. *Time to stretch, push, see exactly what we are capable of.*

"What do you suggest?" Jaxon asked as his mind flitted from one string of numbers to the next.

Pete answered.

"Um, duh, we go down and buy a lottery ticket."

"You want the Powerball numbers, too?"

"Hello? Seriously? Did you really just ask me that?" Pete said incredulously. "Yes, of course."

"Okay. Got them."

Pete leapt to his feet. "Great, let's go."

"Wait, what's going on?" Sadia asked.

"Our genius friend knows the winning lottery numbers. We're going to go buy some tickets."

"Wait for me," Sadia exclaimed.

She ran upstairs and returned moments later with her purse.

"Okay, let's go!"

Jaxon was so busy sorting through all the new information in his head that he walked to the car in a half daze.

"Come on, boy genius," Pete said, finally grabbing him by the shoulder and steering him to the car.

As Pete drove down the street Jaxon stared out the

window. Everything he looked at he could see the math behind. He could tell down to the millimeter how long the block was, he could see in his mind the surface area of the stop sign they passed. He could even tell exactly how many gallons of paint it took to repaint the road the month before.

He didn't have to try and glance at the speedometer to know that the car was traveling at 43.27 miles per hour. He even knew that given the rates at which the lights were cycling it would be 56 seconds faster to take side roads even though it would add 2.9751 miles to the distance. Of course, then he'd have to factor in wear and tear to the tires, rate of gas consumption, and several other things to determine if it would be more cost effective to take the slower, more direct route or to take the longer, faster route.

There were so many numbers and calculations spinning through his head it was nearly overwhelming. It seemed like the whole world was dissolving into numbers: algebra, geometry, probability, calculus, statistics, were coming alive before his very eyes.

He wondered where this power was when he was trying to get through those classes in school. Where had any of it been?

Maybe it was latent until he turned a certain age, it was near his birthday when the real changes started. Maybe it was tied to lunar cycles or the rate at which his cells were replicating and replacing themselves, all of which he knew.

Just as he knew that the cellular reproduction process was accelerating the last few weeks. He blinked rapidly as more numbers seemed to scroll through his eyes. At the rate at which things were going every cell in his body would replace itself within three weeks. That was unprecedented, particularly given that they were supposed to replace themselves at different rates depending on where they were in the body. There was a lot of math behind what was happening. He just needed to push a little harder and-

"Yo, earth to Jaxon!" Pete exclaimed, waving his hand in front of Jaxon's eyes.

Jaxon jumped slightly.

"What?"

"We're here. You totally spaced out again."

"I was just thinking."

"About what?" Sadia asked.

"About more numbers."

"Well, let's get inside before you lose the numbers you already have that we want," Pete said eagerly.

Jaxon slowly got out of the car, squinting slightly. He was trying to avoid looking at too many things and taking in too much information.

We can never have too much information, I have the wisdom to decipher it all.

Jaxon begged to differ. There were some mysteries better left in the universe, including what Sadia's exact dimensions were which he was now all too aware of. He also knew both her and Pete's exact weights.

Which meant he could make a killing as one of those carnival barkers who bet people he could guess their weight. He shook his head. There must be a better use for his newfound skill than that.

Pete hurried him into the convenience store. Inside he dutifully bought one of every lottery ticket he could, including Powerball, Mega Millions, Pick 5, Fantasy 5, and a few others.

"The Pick 5 midday draw is in a few minutes," Sadia said as she read the sign. "So, we'll know shortly if you won."

"The little lady is right," the cashier said. "In ten minutes they'll announce and you can see how you did."

We won.

Jaxon agreed.

His eyes dropped down to the counter. There, under glass, were all the instant win tickets. He crouched down a little lower so he could study each one quickly.

"I'll take Luck of the Irish, Gold Rush, and 2 Hot Cash," Jaxon said, indicating the tickets.

"Absolutely," the cashier said, retrieving the requested scratchers for him. He put them in a bag.

Jaxon took all his tickets and headed back outside with his friends. They climbed into the car.

"Okay, I'm on the website. We should know in six minutes if Jaxon got the Pick 5 right."

He knew they were right and part of him resented her saying "if" as though he could be wrong. He thought about saying something but decided not to. After all, she'd see the truth soon enough.

He handed the Hot Cash scratchers to Sadia.

"It's the second one you want," he said.

"Okay, but I'm scratching both just to make sure."

"Fine."

He handed Pete the Luck of the Irish scratcher and kept the Gold Rush one for himself. Sadia dug into her purse and produced a quarter.

"You go first," Pete said.

She scratched off the first card.

"Nothing on the first," Sadia said, a hint of disappointment in her voice.

Jaxon looked at her. "I already told you that."

"I'm scratching off the second one."

She vigorously scratched for several seconds and then sat, staring at the card, without moving or speaking.

"Well?" Pete finally burst out.

"I won," she said, awe in her voice.

"How much?" Pete asked, craning his neck to try and get a look at her card.

"Twenty-thousand dollars," she stammered.

"Woohoo!" Pete shouted.

He grabbed the quarter from her and went to work on his own scratcher. He blew on it to clear off the extra bits as he finished up.

"Fifty-thousand dollars!" he shouted. He waved the card at both of them. "Do you see that? Fifty-thousand dollars! Jaxon, you're a genius."

Pete practically threw the quarter at him.

"Scratch yours! What did you win?"

Jaxon already knew the answer, but he went through the motions for his friends' sake. He carefully scratched off the winning combination then passed it to Pete to look at.

"Fifteen thousand dollars! You're amazing! This is awesome! We need to go buy more tickets right now."

Jaxon shook his head. "The highest any of the rest of those rolls of scratchers went was a thousand dollars."

"That's still a thousand dollars," Pete said

enthusiastically. "You realize we've got college paid for? Now we need to get matching houses on the same street. What am I saying? Not houses, mansions!"

Jaxon smiled at Pete's enthusiasm. There was a slight twinge of sadness in him, though. Something told him that as much as things were changing, more changes lay ahead for all of them. He didn't want to lose his friends, but in some weird way it almost seemed inevitable that sooner or later he would.

That was all the more reason to enjoy them while he could. He forced a smile back on his face.

"Don't worry, Pete, we've already won enough for our matching mansions," he told him.

"What? How?"

Jaxon held up the stack of lottery tickets he'd gotten.

Pete's eyes bugged out of his head. "I can't believe I forgot! In all the excitement I wasn't even thinking about the winning numbers."

"Well, I was," Sadia said quietly. There was a peculiar tone to her voice. Jaxon could see that she was on her phone staring intently at something.

"What is it?" Jaxon asked.

"The midday draw for the Pick 5."

"He nailed it, didn't he?" Pete asked.

Sadia cleared her throat. "He got all five numbers."

They sat in silence for a moment and then Pete began shouting and pounding the roof of the car.

"Yes, that's my man! He knows all the numbers!"

"You certainly are on a winning streak," Sadia said.

"This isn't a streak. This is the luck of the gods," Pete enthused. "You know what we need to do? Right now?"

Jaxon could sense what his friend was about to say next. He took a deep breath and together with Pete shouted, "Casino!"

Sadia began to laugh hard. She threw up her hands.

"Why not? After all, when you're hot, you're hot, and Jaxon is the hottest," she stuttered to a halt. "With the winning that is, the lucky streak. He's hot that way, that's what I meant. I know it sounded weird-"

"Relax, Sadia," Pete said with a laugh. "And buckle up, because we're headed for the big time!"

You have no idea! Let's see what we can do

* * *

Jaxon had never been inside of a casino before. Neither had Pete or Sadia. He could feel how nervous and excited his friends were as they stepped out of the car in front of the main entrance to a casino attached to a hotel.

The valet rushed forward to collect Pete's keys and Pete grinned like an idiot.

"Take care of her, my good man," he said,

pretending to be rich and snooty and failing miserably because of how much he was smiling.

The valet chuckled, but played along. "Very good, sir."

They walked through the front doors and Jaxon's senses were instantly assaulted. Smoke hung thick in the air, causing him to cough for a second as his lungs weren't used to it. In addition to the smoke there was the smell of alcohol, the metallic scent of a great many coins, sweat, and something else, something more intangible.

"This is cool," Sadia said in awe as she looked around, trying to take in all the sights and sounds at once.

"We're going to clean this place out," Pete said eagerly.

"A little louder, I don't think the mob bosses heard you," Sadia said sarcastically as she glared at Pete.

"This place isn't run by the mob," he protested. "It's like an Indian casino. It's run by tribal elders or something."

"Okay, if you know so much, where should we start?" she asked.

"Well, we can get our feet wet on the slot machines," Pete said. "My grandmother always goes on these bus trips here with other people at her retirement community. She swears by the nickel slot machines, says they bring the bacon home every time."

"I'm not here to play nickel slots," Jaxon said shortly. He shook his head impatiently. That sounded like a waste of time to him.

No, we're not here for the small stuff. We're here to play with the big boys and see how far we can run with this.

"You're Mr. Lucky, you do what you gotta do," Pete said. "As for me, I'm going to find the nickel slots."

A Cashier's cage caught Jaxon's eye and he strode over to it, determined to withdraw some money from his savings account that he opened with the summer gambling winnings Pete gave him from their road trip.

He stood in line and then presented his bank card to the cashier who eyed him dismissively.

"How much you want, kid?" the woman asked in a voice that was deepened by years of smoking.

"I'd like a thousand dollars in chips."

He could tell his request surprised her, but she took his card and a moment later handed it back along with ten one-hundred dollar chips.

"Thanks," he said, stepping aside.

He turned and surveyed the room. His eyes fell on the tables and he moved forward, looking at the various offerings. He saw a craps table and then a baccarat one where a couple of guys were clearly living out some sort of James Bond fantasy.

Finally, he found something that caught his eye. He could see a roulette table, the wheel spinning fast, but not so fast he couldn't still see it clearly. More numbers popped into his head. He was looking at the statistics for winning with the various roulette bets.

I think we can dig our teeth into that.

Jaxon walked up to the roulette table. A casino employee with dark, slicked back hair was running the table. He glanced up as Jaxon approached and looked at him in a dismissive way.

He underestimates us.

Looking around the table Jaxon saw half a dozen players. Each of them reeked of a kind of desperation. Several of them wore fancy clothes and expensive jewelry, but he saw through all of them. They were each standing at that table because they needed a win, a big one, and they were hoping that a little round ball would make all their problems go away. Even if it did make them rich, their problems would still be theirs, though, just slightly different.

Jaxon had a stack of chips in his hand that represented a thousand dollars. He stood for a moment, watching as the ball spun round and round before bouncing out of the twenty-three and into the five slot.

"Five red," the croupier with the slicked back hair said.

Everyone at the table groaned and scowled as they watched him slide all their chips off the numbered mat and into the house's bank.

The players grudgingly put forward more chips, each no doubt covering a favored number.

Jaxon let his hand hover in the air for a moment. He was waiting for the *inner* voice to tell him that which he already instinctively felt.

Eight.

Yes, that was it.

Jaxon dropped his entire stack of chips onto the table, on the eight square.

Always bet on eight.

"Young man, you might want to reconsider betting everything you have in such a reckless fashion," a woman who was old enough to be his grandmother admonished him.

"Fortunately, I'm not reckless," he said softly.

"Jaxon, you're crazy," Sadia said as she moved up beside him and eyed his bet with wide eyes.

"You think so, really? After everything?" he asked quietly.

She turned to look at him and blinked a couple of times.

We're melting her brain. She can't deal with it.

Jaxon took a deep breath and then forced himself to give her a small smile. He wished she understood, but she didn't. She was still struggling to catch up, to figure out what was going on with him.

"Betting is closed," the croupier said.

Jaxon turned back to watch as the metal ball begin spinning rapidly around the wheel. He didn't have to watch. He already knew what was going to happen. Still, he might as well watch his victory.

The ball circled lower and lower, then hit the wheel. It bounced crazily from one number to another until finally settling.

"Eight black!" the croupier exclaimed.

People around the table burst out in loud exclamations.

The croupier pushed Jaxon's money onto the table. Thirty-five thousand was what he'd won.

The smart move was to take the money and run, not walk, away. There were also safer bets he could make or he could choose a new number completely. He knew better, though.

"Let it ride," he said.

"Sir, the table limit is five-thousand," the croupier protested.

Sadia tugged on his arm. "Take it and let's go," she whispered.

"I'd listen to your girlfriend, young man," the old woman said.

"She's not my girlfriend and has anyone ever gotten good advice from you?" he asked.

"Jaxon!" Sadia gasped. "Be nice to the lady," she added, lowering her voice.

Sadia stared at him like he'd lost his mind. He just turned back to the croupier.

"I'm sure you could clear it with the floor manager," he said.

The croupier signaled for someone and a moment later a tall, brunette woman with her hair pulled back in a severe bun approached the table. She was wearing a tailored black suit with her white shirt unbuttoned lower than it could be for any other type of business establishment. Jaxon caught a glimpse of a lace bra as she moved up close and bent slightly over the table.

She's showing off on purpose. It's her way to distract and intimidate, his *inner* voice warned him.

From the looks on the faces of the other players, it was certainly working on them.

The croupier shared a few quiet words with the pit boss then turned to look at Jaxon.

"Well, Mr…"

"You can call me Jaxon," he said.

"Mr. Jaxon, it is against our house policy to allow single bets of this size. Five thousand per bet is the table limit. I would be willing to extend that for you, but only up to ten."

With a great show Jaxon picked up ten thousand and dropped it on black. He then picked up another ten thousand and dropped it on even. He picked up five thousand and dropped it on the corner where 7-8-10-11 intersected. He left the remaining ten thousand on 8 then he stared at the pit boss.

She pursed her lips and narrowed her eyes, clearly not amused. She also clearly wanted to see him lose so after a moment she nodded her head slightly.

"All bets in," the croupier said.

Two of the other players scrambled to shove their chips onto the 8 along with Jaxon's.

"Betting is closed," the croupier said.

The little metal ball went whirling. This time Jaxon didn't bother looking at the wheel. Instead he stared straight into the eyes of the pit boss. He felt like he was almost daring her to break eye contact to look at the wheel.

First one blinks, loses.

She was tough and was clearly used to dealing with

tough players. She held eye contact, not flinching even as they could hear the metal ball bounce from one number to another.

The bouncing sound suddenly stopped. There was the briefest of pauses, as if the world was holding its breath.

"Eight black," the croupier croaked.

"What?" the pit boss snapped, dropping her eyes to the wheel.

Jaxon smiled to himself.

The bets on even and black were a wash as they only had a 1 to 1 pay out. The 5,000 bet on the corners paid out $40,000. The 10,000 on 8 paid out $350,000.

At the revelation, the players around him broke into spontaneous applause and several others nearby came hurrying over to see what had happened.

"Congratulations. Let me take you to the cashier," the pit boss said in a tone of voice that let him know she wouldn't take no for an answer.

"Lead on," he said.

Five minutes later he had the original ten thousand he started with, plus a cashier's check for $400,000. Sadia, who accompanied him, quickly shoved it in her purse then proceeded to clutch it as a drowning man would a life preserver.

"Relax," he told her. "If we lose it there's plenty more to find."

"That's easy for you to say."

"Yes, actually it is."

"We should go find Pete and get out of here."

"What are you talking about?" he asked her with a shake of his head. "We're just getting started."

"Can we at least go find Pete? I'm hungry. Maybe we can get something to eat?" she asked, eyes and voice pleading.

"Where did you last see him?" Jaxon asked.

"He was playing one of the slot machines with a progressive jackpot over there," she said, waving off to the left.

Jaxon started walking in that direction. He passed row after row of shiny machines with bright displays and blinking lights. He caught the reflection of his *inner* self smiling at him as they passed every chrome bank.

There was more, though. He realized that the machines were talking. There were a lot of beeps, whistles, and clangs interspersed with the occasional sound of an alarm going off or coins being spit out. This was different. It was a sound that was lying beneath all of that noise. There was a series of low frequency clicks, not that dissimilar from the sound an old-fashioned typewriter made only much lower in pitch and softer in volume.

He listened for a few moments and then he knew what they were saying. More importantly, he could tell which machines were ready to pay out.

"There he is!" Sadia exclaimed, ruining his concentration.

She was pointing to the next row over where Pete sat, shoulders hunched, in front of one of the loudest screaming bandits in the entire place. He was sweating and his hair was plastered to his forehead. He was clutching a bucket of coins, cradling it to his body as he pulled one out, put it into the machine, then pulled the trigger.

Two 7s and a banana showed up.

Jaxon shook his head. It would take Pete hours playing that way on that machine before the thing started to pay off and he'd be so hopelessly in the hole at that point that he'd be unable to crawl out.

On the other hand, the machine to Pete's left was sending out all kinds of signals. Jaxon closed his eyes for a moment, listening to the clicks and working to interpret them.

Satisfied, he opened his eyes. He fished around in his pocket for a coin and then stepped up to the machine.

"Pete."

His friend turned and looked at him with eyes that were already bloodshot from the smoke in the air.

"Yeah?" Pete asked, his voice slightly dazed.

"Have you tried this one?" Jaxon asked.

"No, you think I should?"

Jaxon made a show of putting the coin into the machine. Then he pulled the lever and stepped back. The wheels began spinning wildly.

Diamond.

Diamond.

Diamond.

Pete screamed and jumped up and down as the call button on the top of the machine lit up and bells started clanging.

"Do me a favor? Take Sadia to the buffet," Jaxon said.

He turned and walked off.

"Jaxon!" Sadia called after him, but he didn't turn around. In the background Pete was still yelling in excitement.

He had important things to do and he didn't need the distraction. Two minutes later he made it out of the maze of slot machines and saw more table games. He sidled up to a blackjack table, found an open chair, and took a seat.

The dealer was just starting a new hand. He looked up at Jaxon and nodded as Jaxon slid a thousand dollar chip onto the table.

Jaxon won the first three hands easily enough. The fourth one the dealer gave him two aces to start with. Jaxon immediately split them, upping his bet. His mind was racing as he calculated the odds, factoring in the cards that had already made an appearance.

The dealer was showing an eleven. It was possible he had a ten face down. He dealt Jaxon a queen on his first ace. On his second he dealt him a six. Normally seventeen would be a good hand to stand on, but Jaxon wasn't there to pull his punches. He tapped that hand and the dealer dealt him a four.

"Double blackjack," the dealer said when Jaxon flipped over his cards.

That brought Jaxon's stack of chips to twenty-five thousand. Just then a middle-aged man with an expensive suit approached the table and addressed Jaxon.

"Good day, sir. Allow me to introduce myself. I'm Max and I handle accounts for our high rollers here at the casino."

"Okay," Jaxon asked.

"I've taken the liberty of enrolling you in our rewards program."

"How, you don't know my name?"

The man smiled faintly. "Don't worry, sir, we are quite good at taking care of our high rollers. I know who you are Mr. Jaxon."

"That's actually my first name."

"I know."

"Thanks, but I'm not sure I'm going to be a regular," Jaxon said, trying to dismiss the man.

Wait, let's see if he can challenge us, his *inner* voice said.

"We hope to change your mind about that. I can see that you are a man of action. I respect that. I'm here to offer you something that you can't get here on the floor."

"And what's that?" Jaxon asked warily.

"You've been invited to a very special game," Max said. "One designed to cater to our high rollers."

"Excuse me?" Jaxon said.

"If you would follow me, we have something that I think you'll find much more… stimulating."

Jaxon reluctantly picked up his stacks of chips, turned, and followed the man.

"Dude, where are they taking you?" Pete whispered as he suddenly came up alongside.

"Hopefully, somewhere interesting."

"How much money has he won?" Sadia asked.

"A lot," Pete said.

"He should quit while he's ahead," she said.

"I'm not done yet," Jaxon said without turning to look at her.

He followed the man to a closed door on the far side of the casino. The man turned to him, nodded, and then opened the door and escorted him into a small room where five other men sat around a poker table. A female dealer with blonde hair, blue eyes, and a sly smile was flexing her fingers over a deck of cards.

Pete and Sadia started to follow him, but Max held

up a hand.

"Players only," the man said shortly.

"Jaxon?" Sadia asked questioningly.

"I'll be fine. I'll beat these guys and then I'll see you in a little bit."

"Dude, you want to be-"

Jaxon didn't hear the rest of whatever Pete was trying to tell him as Max gently but firmly pushed him and Sadia out of the room with him, closing the door behind him.

Cards were scattered across the table and each man had a massive pile of chips in front of him. Eyeing the pot in the middle of the table, Jaxon guessed it to be at ten-thousand dollars.

It seemed he'd found himself invited into a high-stakes poker game.

"So, you're the guy that's been burning up the tables," a Texan with a large mustache said as he visibly sized Jaxon up.

"Pull up a chair, boy," the man said.

*Been playing since he was a kid on his dad's knee.
Been in tournaments all over the world. We've seen his
face before.*

Jaxon nodded and slowly took a seat at an empty
place.

The man next to him, who had a distinctly European
look, scooted his chair several inches away with a
distasteful grimace on his face.

He doesn't like us.

Jaxon didn't need the guy to like him. He just needed
the other man to lose.

"Stop hoarding your gold like some fool dragon," a
man across the table snapped at him. The man was
wearing a geeky T-shirt underneath a sports jacket that
was expensive but rumpled.

Tech guy. He'll know the odds. He'll attack the game

with logic, even if he is wearing a fantasy shirt.

Jaxon realized he was still holding onto his winnings. He slowly, purposefully, put it all down on the table with a thud.

That got the attention of the remaining two players at the table. The first one looked up and Jaxon realized he had seen his face on billboards around town. The man was a state senator running for reelection.

Professional liar. He'll be a master of the bluff.

The senator stared at him, eyes narrowed, then pursed his lips and nodded slightly.

Jaxon guessed that meant he had been accepted.

The fifth man was staring at him intently from behind a pair of dark sunglasses. He was careful to hide his eyes. The weeks worth of beard somehow seemed out of place on the man, and Jaxon finally realized why.

The fifth player was Trent Stewart, a famous actor that Sadia and half the girls at his school had been

136

crushing on since the fifth grade.

"Trent, your turn," the Texan barked.

Trent dropped his eyes back to the table and he hastily picked up a few chips and tossed them into the pile.

At that the European shoved his cards forward in disgust.

Jaxon continued to eye the move star thoughtfully, waiting to hear what his *inner* voice had to say about Trent.

He's rich and bored. He doesn't care if he loses. He doesn't even really care if he wins. That makes him the most dangerous man at the table. There was a pause then the *inner* voice continued. *Except for us.*

Jaxon was ready.

Poker was just as much about strategy as it was about the cards dealt. On his first hand, Jaxon ended up with a full house, queens over sixes. Still, when he called the

Texan's bluff and the man revealed three kings, Jaxon dropped his hand into the discard pile without revealing that he had actually won.

He wanted to see how each of the men he was playing with handled themselves, how they bet, when they bluffed. It took him less than fifteen minutes to pick up on each of their tells.

Trent was the hardest to read, partly because he was an actor and partly because he just really didn't care. He was there to play and winning or losing were incidental. At last Jaxon got a handle on him, too.

On the next hand, Jaxon was dealt two aces. The draw gave him the other two. He didn't smile. He was careful not to express any emotion whatsoever as he raised the pot fifteen-thousand.

The Texan gave a long, low whistle, and tossed in his hand. Everyone else stayed in. When it came around to the European, he raised which forced out the politician and the tech guy. That left Jaxon, Trent, and the European in. Jaxon raised the stakes again, and both men matched him with the European finally calling him.

"Four aces," Jaxon said, flipping over his cards.

Pandemonium broke out in the room. Jaxon grinned to himself as he raked in the pot.

Time to go.

Jaxon shook his head. He had no intention of going. He was having fun and he was just getting started.

We've done everything we can here. There's no challenges left. Let's go. I'm bored.

Again, Jaxon refused to listen. This was one time his *inner* voice was not going to get the final say. He was enjoying playing for the high stakes and outwitting all those who thought themselves older and wiser.

Jaxon played three more hands, then managed to come up with a royal flush. At that point two of the other players got up and stormed off.

"Sore losers," Jaxon said with a smirk.

Moments later two huge, burly security guards entered the room.

"Mr. Jaxon?"

"Yes?" he asked.

"Miss Janis wants to see you."

He believed Janis was the pit boss he had encountered earlier.

"Tell her in a minute," he said with a sigh.

"No one makes the boss wait. Please get up."

The dealer and the remaining players all looked askance at Jaxon. With an exaggerated show of frustration he gathered up his winnings, stood, and followed the two goons.

They took him through a series of doors away from the main casino and in less than a minute he was standing in an office where Janis was waiting. He was surprised to find that Pete and Sadia were already there, both of them looking a little guilty and scared.

"I don't know how you're doing it, Mr. Jaxon," the lady boss said coldly.

"Doing what?" he asked.

"Cheating. I can't see how, but I know that no one is that lucky. So, if you don't mind, I'd like you and your friends to leave now."

"I'm not cheating," Jaxon protested.

Come on, I'm bored, let's go.

"Sure you're not," she said sarcastically.

He didn't know why he wanted to argue with the woman, but it rubbed him the wrong way to be called a cheater when he wasn't.

"I didn't cheat at a single one of those games. I just know how to play them."

"Look, I'm not here to argue with you. Take your winnings and go quietly. Otherwise, I'll be forced to call the police," she said with a raised eyebrow.

"Let it go, man," Pete said, clearly concerned.

"Come on, Jaxon. Enough is enough," Sadia said.

He set his jaw as he reflected that nothing was ever enough. He certainly hadn't had his fill of winning yet.

Let's get out of here. There's nothing interesting left to do, his *inner* self urged.

"Fine," Jaxon said. He had a couple of cashier's checks in Sadia's purse and a roll of hundred dollar bills in his pocket thick enough to choke a horse.

Two hulking security guards insisted on walking them out. Jaxon just rolled his eyes, knowing that neither of them could do anything about it if he decided not to leave on his own.

The guards walked with them all the way to the exit and waited until the valet had brought around the car.

"We need to get a new car," Jaxon commented as they all climbed in.

"Yes, please," Pete said quickly.

Once they were inside Sadia leaned forward. "Where are we going now?"

"I've got a lot of cash to burn. Why don't we go to a bar?" Jaxon said.

"Now there's a great idea!" Pete said enthusiastically.

"Ummm…geniuses… we're going to get kicked out of there faster than we got kicked out of the casino. Last time I checked, none of us has a fake i.d.," Sadia said.

Jaxon chuckled. "Who needs a fake i.d. when you have lots of money?"

"I've heard my cousins talk about this place, called the Fifth Dimension. It's a couple of miles from here," Pete said.

"What are we waiting for?" Jaxon asked.

Pete drove to the club and they had to park two blocks away. The street the Fifth Dimension was on seemed to be filled with other bars and clubs. It gave an intense, edgy vibe to the whole area. People were coming and going, some alone, others with dates they could barely keep their hands off of.

They reached the front of the bar and an intense looking bouncer eyed them suspiciously.

"I.D.," he said perfunctorily.

"Sure," Jaxon said. "Here's mine, and my two friends'." He held out three hundred-dollar bills.

The man narrowed his eyes then took the bills, eyed them for a moment, and then stuffed them into his pocket.

"Have a good time and don't draw attention to yourselves," he said.

"Wouldn't dream of it," Jaxon said with a serene smile.

They walked inside and were instantly immersed in a world of pulsing lights and pounding music. They made their way to the bar having to shimmy past gyrating bodies on the dance floor to do so.

"This place is crazy!" Pete shouted.

"Yeah," Jaxon muttered.

The music was so loud that it was giving his heightened sense of hearing a problem. Within a minute his head was pounding.

Once they made it to the bar Sadia ordered a tequila sunrise, Pete ordered a beer, and Jaxon briefly wondered if he could order aspirin. He ended up opting for a shot of vodka. The liquid burned his throat as it went down.

He turned and surveyed the rest of the club. There were people dancing or at least swaying to the music everywhere with bodies packed nearly shoulder-to-shoulder.

Lots of desperate people drowning themselves in noise and booze.

He had to agree with his *inner* voice. He did, however, like the pleasant sensation of the vodka in his system. He ordered a second one and found that the burn wasn't as bad as the first had been.

"You wanna dance?" Sadia asked, practically having to shout to make herself heard.

"Where?" he asked, indicating the mass of people.

"Good point!" she shouted back.

"Let's go someplace else," Jaxon said.

"I'm not done with my beer," Pete protested.

"I'll get you another somewhere else."

They made it back out of the club and the bouncer glanced at them in surprise.

"Can you recommend somewhere a bit quieter?" Jaxon asked.

The man chuckled. "That's a first. Yeah, Lucky Libations, half a block up."

"Thanks, man."

The three of them walked up the street and quickly found the place. It was more of a traditional bar, but

Jaxon's hundred-dollar bills were just as effective on the bartender there.

"At least I can hear myself think again," Sadia said.

The pounding in Jaxon's head was subsiding and the alcohol he'd already consumed was making him feel a bit more relaxed.

"Yeah, that other place was a bit much," he admitted.

Pete shrugged. "I said it was popular, not that it was good."

Jaxon smiled as the bartender handed all three of them Jell-o shots. The liquor infused Jell-o slid easily down his throat and he quickly followed it up with two more.

"That stuff will sneak up on you," the bartender warned.

Jaxon shrugged. What did he care? After all, he was invincible in every other way, why not this as well?

July 24, 2018br

2:51 am

They hung out in Lucky Libations for about half an hour before heading to the pub two doors down. In there, Sadia and Pete scarfed down a giant plate of nachos. Jaxon wasn't hungry, but he was enjoying sampling the different types of drinks the bartender kept serving up to them.

An hour later, he was starting to really feel the effects. Sadia and Pete both urged him to eat something to help soak up the alcohol, but he didn't feel like it.

Although part of him was having a good time, most of him was bored and restless. The *inner* self kept urging him to go do something interesting. Every time it did, he took another shot in an attempt to drown it out.

"This is interesting," he said, slurring his words slightly.

Not to me.

"You're being no fun," he insisted.

You're the one wasting time on trivial pursuits. We need to be challenging ourselves, pushing ourselves.

"I am challenging myself. I'm challenging myself to drink as much as I possibly can," Jaxon said.

At least pick someone to outdrink, a sailor or something.

"There's no one here who looks like they can hold their liquor," Jaxon said.

Bored.

"Lighten up."

Waste of time.

"I'm having fun with my friends."

Really? Where are they?

The *inner* self had a good point. Jaxon swiveled his

head around, looking for them. Pete was sitting next to an older woman, eagerly buying her another round of drinks. It was clear from the look on his friend's face what he was hoping to get out of it.

Jaxon raised his glass in a toast.

"To you, Mrs. Robinson," he said.

Sadia was talking to what looked like a college guy who was openly ogling her. Jaxon felt an unexpected pang of irritation. He got up and walked unsteadily over to her.

"Time to go," he said.

Sadia looked at him in surprise.

"What's the rush?" she asked.

"We need to clear our head," he said.

She frowned but nodded. She turned back to the guy she'd been talking to.

"I'm sorry. I have to go."

"At least give me your digits," the guy urged.

Sadia dropped her eyes. "Sorry," she muttered.

She grabbed her sweater and marched toward the door.

"Pete! We're going!" she shouted.

Pete started up. He looked from them to the woman he was attempting to charm then back again. He flushed red then with a heavy sigh he walked toward them.

"You know you totally ruined that? She was into me," he complained when he reached them at the door.

"She was into all those drinks you bought her," Sadia countered.

"Well, as long as I was part of the equation somewhere," he grumbled.

"Let's go," Jaxon said, heading out the door.

"Where?" Sadia asked. "Home?"

"Another bar?" Pete asked hopefully. "Ideally one with even hotter, more desperate women?"

"You're disgusting," Sadia said.

Pete shrugged. "Beggars can't be choosers, but we can still dream."

Jaxon was growing tired of the inane prattle. He was itching for something. He just didn't know what it was.

"Hey, dude, be careful!" Pete called.

Jaxon ignored him as he stepped off the curb into the street. A moment later he heard the honking sound of a foghorn. Out of the corner of his eye he saw lights bearing down on him. He blinked trying to see what was coming and realized he should get out of the way. He tried, but it was too late.

A dump truck hit him full on, sending him flying. He hit the pavement and rolled several times. His head smacked against the ground hard before blacking out.

* * *

The dump truck's tires were spinning as the driver

stood on the brakes. He needn't have bothered. After all, the force of the impact brought the vehicle to an immediate stop, as if he just hit an immovable object. The driver looked over the steering wheel to see a man partially wrapped in the front of his truck staring back at him.

He stared up at the truck driver and shook his head in anger slowly to indicate his displeasure, as he started to unwedged himself.

"You should've been watching where you were going".

The driver just stared at him, mouth agape, as though he had seen a ghost. He was completely confused about what just happened. He couldn't remember anything that lead up to the accident, all he could say was he was sorry, and are you ok?

The man quickly examined his body for injuries, with his blurry vision he just stared at his hands looking confused.

Sadia and Pete ran pass him and the truck, both shouting and screaming.

Wondered where they were going, he say's

"Guys, I'm fine,"

"I feel amazing, clearheaded, sober".

The sensation of air on his skin was a little more heightened than it normally was and his senses, particularly his vision, seemed to get sharper somehow, better. He was also stronger. Given that everything had been improving lately it was a bit startling to find that there was an even greater level of power and awareness he was feeling.

Sadia and Pete were crouched on the ground, still yelling. It didn't make any sense. He walked over to them with a frown.

"Pete, Sadia, I'm fine," he said once he was hovering over them.

They both jerked their heads upward then looked at him in confusion.

"*Hey, what's the problem?*" he asked.

"Who are you, Mister?" Pete asked.

"Can you call an ambulance for our friend? He was hit by that truck," Sadia said as tears started to course down her cheeks.

"*Um, yeah, I know. I'm fine.*"

"Who are you?" Pete asked.

He laughed.

"*What do you mean? Quit clowning around Pete. It's me, Jaxon.*"

Pete shook his head.

"I don't know you, Mister. And you're certainly not my friend Jaxon."

"*How can you say that?*" he asked.

Then he looked past Pete and Sadia to the body lying in blood crumpled on the ground. They must know him from the fuss they were making. He took a step forward to get a better look and suddenly he recognized himself. That was his body, sprawled out unconscious.

He looked down at himself again, but slowly this time. The skin on his hands was olive. He lifted them slowly and felt his face. The features were wrong, different.

No, not wrong. He *was*, we are, Jaxon. And lying unmoving on the ground was…his outer self.

"*You can see me?*" he asked.

"Of course we can see you. Who are you?" Pete asked.

He slowly lifted his hand to his throat and the necklace that he'd been wearing for as long as he could remember. He fiddled with the familiar edges of the seven point star, including the odd little extra point. He'd had it all his life and it was with him even now.

The necklace was there as was the raised patch of

skin on his neck that was his birthmark. He crouched down next to the body on the ground and moved his hand to the throat. He was surprised to find that the pale skin beneath his fingers was cold to the touch. The Jaxon unconscious on the ground had neither the necklace nor the birthmark.

He wasn't the only one who noticed. Sadia suddenly gave out a shriek and scrambled backward several steps.

"Who… who are you?" she gasped.

"*Jaxon*," he said.

"Sadia, this guy's just tripping, ignore him," Pete urged.

Out there, somewhere, there is something, a powerful force that is emerging into this realm. It's interesting in its own way because it is new, unknown. That interest is not enough to move me, but that does not mean I am unmoved. For I know there is a location, a place, where we will meet in this realm. It is inevitable, we will both arrive together.

An ant may walk for half its life and not cover the ground a man may walk in a single day. A man may walk many miles and think himself having undertaken a lengthy journey that would be despised by larger, faster creatures. It is not the distance that is at issue, but the perspective.

Distance may be deceptive because perception of it can be influenced by purpose. Walking a long distance to find food, water, shelter, or other necessities might seem like grueling work that makes every step feel like a thousand. Yet, that same distance, when traversed for purposes of joy, pleasure, or companionship can seem short indeed and our eager steps make quick work of its passing. The distance itself has not changed, but rather we ourselves are changed in our attitude toward it.

I do not know how great a distance separates this new entity from myself. I do not know how long the journey that it will take or that I will before our paths reach that point of intersection, that crossroads where we will first meet each other. I do not know if it will cross that distance with anticipation or dread of what it might discover when it reaches its destination. For myself, I will restrain judgment, and allow myself to feel a sense of mild curiosity that will allow the miles to pass not unpleasantly, but with no great hurry.

Chapter 4

God Parents

Aug 25, 2000br

District of Columbia

Streaks of morning light softened as they passed through the thin gossamer curtain. The golden flecks in Jenna's tanned skin caught the light as she stretched. Jenna yawned with each stretch and rolled onto her side. Faint sounds filled the air. She sat up, and her eyes sprung open.

"What's that?"

Julius entered from the bathroom with a towel wrapped around his waist.

"Our son. You wanna have a go at making another one?" Julius crawled into bed and leaned in for a kiss. Jenna gathered the sheets up around her and jerked away from his reach.

"What's wrong with you? We playing keep away?" Julius chuckled.

"What did you do to me?" Jenna's leg tangled up in the sheets as she slid back. She fell backward.

Julius grabbed her arm attempting to save her from the floor.

"I'm all for role playing but this is a bit much."

Jenna pushed Julius away.

"Get off me." The sheets flew up and Jenna hit the floor hard. "Ouch."

Julius leaned over the edge of the bed, concerned.

"What's wrong with you?"

Cries fill the room. "I'm hungry."

Julius grabbed the baby monitor.

"Who else is here?" Jenna backed herself and the sheets into a corner hoping for some sort of protection.

Julius shook his head.

"Our son, remember?" Julius rushed out of the room.

Jenna pulled her knees to her chest. Her body shook. Son, what was going on? Jenna wracked her brain trying to figure out how she could have a son. She scanned the room, unfamiliar with her surroundings. Her gazed stopped on a picture of her and a smiling Julius in wedding attire on the nightstand. She cautiously pushed the closet open with her foot. All her clothes were there.

She yanked out a pair of pants and hoody. In a panic she jammed her feet in the pants and pulled the hoody on. She stuffed her feet in a pair of shoes. She grabbed the photo and ran to the door. Julius bounced a baby boy in his arms and he stopped at the threshold of the bedroom. Jenna halted at the sight of him.

"Move." She said.

"You're freaking me out," he replied.

"What's going on, what is this?" Jenna held up the wedding photo.

Julius stared at Jenna, perplexed.

"Our wedding day."

"No, no, no, no! We just started dating."

Jenna tried to squeeze past Julius and the baby.

"Are you crazy, you'll hurt him." Julius shifted his weight and forced the baby into Jenna's arms. "Stop. Let me get dressed and we'll figure this out."

She took the baby and sat on the edge of the bed awkwardly trying to control the movements of the child.

He smiled at Jenna. "Mommy pretty."

"Did he?…"

"He's smart." Julius said as he pulled on a pair of sweats.

"He's just a baby." Jenna forced a smile. He couldn't have been more than a couple months old. How could he speak?"

"Hold him while I get his food."

Julius rushed out and disappeared down the hallway.

Jenna laid the baby down. He sat up and reached for her. She craned her neck checking for her so-called husband to return. The baby maneuvered to his feet. He reached out for her and took step after step toward her. She cringed at his approach.

"How are you doing that?"

Jenna held her hand out to the baby. He smiled and giggled. A grin overtook her face.

"It's just a baby. He can't hurt you."

Julius rounded the corner with a spoon and baby food in hand.

"It's feeding time, Jaxon."

Jenna yanked her hand back. Jaxon fell back and

burst into tears.

"Jaxon." She whispered his name, trying it out. It seemed familiar.

Julius sat on the bed. He lifted Jaxon into his arms and scooted back till his back rested against the headboard. He cracked the jar open and handed Jaxon the spoon.

Jaxon took hold of the spoon and dug into his jar. He had the dexterity of a much older child. Each spoonful found his mouth with ease. He reached out for Jenna. "Mom, I want mom."

She gasped. "This isn't real."

What was she seeing? This had to be a dream. Her gaze meandered. Her mouth fell open at the sight of a birthmark on Jaxon's neck.

"He prefers you, can't say I blame him." Julius chuckled to himself. He looked to Jenna. "You don't remember anything?"

She sprung from the bed.

"No. He's not mine. I don't know what's going on but I've never been pregnant."

Julius's face sank.

"Look at your stomach. Your breasts."

Jenna turned away from him. She moved her hand down to her stomach. Her mind raced. It was bigger than she remembered. She yanked up her shirt and saw stretch marks, and moved her hand up to her breast and winced at the pain.

"You haven't pumped today. You usually do it after your shower." Julius pulled the spoon from Jaxon and wiped his mouth.

"This isn't real." A tremble started in her hands and moved throughout her entire body.

Julius laid Jaxon on the bed. In two swift moves Julius moved from the bed to Jenna. He wrapped his arms around her. She sank into his warmth.

"I don't know what's going on but we'll figure this out together," he said as he kissed her neck.

She squirmed from his grasp.

"No!"

Julius reached out to her.

"I know you're scared."

Shaking her head wildly.

"You're lying."

"I am your husband; we've been together over a year."

"I would remember you and him."

"But you don't. Let me take you to the hospital."

"No, I wanna go home."

"But..."

"Take me home, now!"

Julius's six-foot-four frame sagged as he exhaled.

"Okay, then we get you checked out." Julius nodded at Jenna until she followed suit. Once he was sure they were in agreement he picked up Jaxon.

"Please stay here. I just need a few minutes to get him ready."

* * *

Jenna wondered what was really going on. What if he was telling the truth? Had she really lost time? If so, how much? The room was filled with her things. Photos of her and this man. Her phone. Why hadn't she thought of that first? Jenna scrambled to the bedside table. She grabbed her phone. It was the same. She typed in the password. It didn't work. She told herself to slow down. She took a breath and tried again. Still nothing. She only had one more try. Jenna tossed the phone aside. Panic overtook her again. This wasn't real. She wrapped her arms around herself. He said he would take her home. Olivia would be there and help her make sense of this. She just needed to relax. She was going home.

* * *

Julius sat behind the wheel of a sleek minivan. His head swiveled like an automated fan between the road, a view of Jaxon in the rearview mirror, and Jenna.

Jaxon played happily with the toys that hung from his handle. He waved at his reflection in the mirror.

"Let's play."

"He does that sometimes," Julius commented as he continued his pointed glares from the road to Jenna, to Jaxon.

Wow. How was she supposed to be a mother to a child who was so advanced? With each glance Jenna's irritation grew. She took to biting her nails. She tried closing her eyes, but she could feel his glares. She wished he'd stop looking at her like she was some wounded animal.

"Can you stop?" she finally burst out.

"Sorry, I've never seen you do that before."

"Sit in a car?"

"Bite your nails."

"I do it when I'm nervous, if we were married you'd know that."

Julius let out a hearty laugh.

"That's still the same. Blunt as ever."

Jenna rolled her eyes.

"Stop it, you don't know me."

Observing the stop sign, Julius slowed to a stop.

"I'm Julius, Jenna. You know me."

Jenna's face softened.

"You keep saying you know me, but we just started dating."

Julius smirked.

"You remember." He pulled through the intersection

and rejoined traffic.

Shaking her head.

"No, I remember O... my friend set us up. But... I never..." Jenna's heart quickened. She struggled to breathe. Jenna grabbed the door handle and yanked at it. The doors were locked. He had locked her in. She pushed the button, but it didn't unlock the door. She couldn't breathe, so she pulled at the lock itself.

Julius leaned over to grab her.

"Stop it, are you trying to kill yourself?"

"Let me out. You drugged and kidnapped me." As tears streamed down her face. "You're sick. You put something in my drink and... made me have that."

Julius yanked the wheel. He pulled into a parking lot slammed on the breaks and cut off the car.

"I get it. You're freaked out. You don't know me or him. But you looked around the house. What about that makes you think you'd been hurt in any way?"

Jenna opened her mouth ready to argue. She thought back to the room she woke up in. Her things were arranged lovingly. Her favorite artwork hung in the living room. Her body sagged.

"I know you don't have any reason to trust me, but I'm taking you to Olivia, maybe you'll trust her. Then we can find out what's going on. Okay?"

Jenna stiffened. She had no choice. She had no money and no idea where she was. Julius took her silence as agreement. He restarted the car and pulled back into traffic. She leaned back and watched the cars and landscape speed by. She noted the new construction. Everything seemed so familiar but different. She turned to Julius. He genuinely seemed concerned and hurt at her accusation. He knew Olivia. What did that mean? Jenna figured it was better not to think about it, at least for now. There would be plenty of time for all that. Her body felt rested but mentally she was depleted. Jenna allowed her eyes to close and she drifted off to dreamland. Hopefully, she'd wake up and find that this ordeal had been the real dream.

***

Julius's mind sped through possible reasons for what was going on. He'd done a Google search and what he'd found alarmed him. He watched Jenna closely looking for signs of illness. For the first time he prayed. Not just that Jenna would be okay but also that she would go to the doctor to figure out what was going on.

***

Jenna found herself slumped in the passenger's seat. She turned to find him driving in silence. Her wish had not come true. Julius was still there. Which meant this was no nightmare. Jenna could feel his stare boring into her. She felt the car slow and come to a halt.

She sat up and exhaled. They were at her apartment. Her and Olivia's. They'd lived together since college. Jenna turned to Julius. He brought her home. Just like he said. Jenna reached for the handle but stopped. The click of the door unlocking filled the space. Jenna flung the door open. She ran up the stairs and pulled on the door. She needed a key. She hadn't thought about that.

She looked to the left. The intercom was missing. In its place was a panel to punch in a security code. When was that installed? Jenna felt so close to answers but yet another roadblock had been thrown at her. Now what?

Julius came up beside her with a sleeping Jaxon in his arms. When did he get out of the car? She hadn't heard anything. No footsteps. No car door. Much less two. Julius punched in a code: two, two, three, seven, nine. The door beeped. Jenna stared at him in disbelief.

How did he know?

"Olivia gave it to me. I wanted to make sure she was home. She's waiting for you. We'll stay out here."

Jaxon reached out to Jenna.

"Momma, come back."

Jenna yanked the door open and ran inside. She didn't dare look back as she entered the apartment building on a mission. She could only go forward. Whatever that child was it couldn't be hers. He was just too much. The world had gone mad. No! Jenna shook her head. She needed something she could grasp onto. All she needed was to find Olivia. Olivia would make the world right again. Make it all make sense.

* * *

Jenna found herself pressed against the elevator doors waiting for them to open. The waiting was driving her mad.

Had they always been this slow? Jenna's hand trembled. She exhaled every bit of air in her lungs and took in a deep breath and repeated. She had just started a sleep app the night before. No, not the night before. A year ago. No, more. The baby was three months old. How long had it really been? No, she couldn't go down the rabbit hole. Not yet. Breathe. Focus on the breath. That was how to relax the body in times of stress. It helped one sleep. But sleep wasn't her aim. She had apparently done a year's worth of that.

The breathing exercises were starting to work. Her hand was now still. And with that, the elevator beeped and the doors slid open. She almost fell into the hallway and all that breath work went out the window. Jenna's heart quickened with each step toward the apartment. Olivia was there behind the door. Olivia would tell her what was going on.

"Olivia."

Jenna balled her fist and exhaled. She tapped out her

standard five knocks. It felt weird to do this on her own door. Jenna heard nothing. She raised her hand again and the door peeled back as she burst into tears.

"Olivia."

Olivia, a dark chocolate woman with an afro, wrapped her arms around Jenna and held her tight.

"I got you."

The two sank to the floor and sat for what Jenna wished was an eternity. Because in those moments Jenna was home.

A little while later Jenna stared out the window. She was transfixed on the pouring rain. She hoped Julius had enough sense to get the baby in the car or better yet home.

"Jen, your tea."

Jenna turned around to find a smiling Olivia with a cup of piping hot tea in her hand. This was exactly what she needed. Olivia sat on the couch and waited for Jenna to join her. When Jenna finally did she couldn't find the words. She was just so happy to be around familiarity. Although the place wasn't exactly that. The drapes, table, and microwave were all new.

Olivia took the tea from Jenna and sat it on the coffee table and took her friend's hand. "Did something happen with you and Julius? Is Jax okay?"

Jenna jerked her hand away from Olivia and picked the tea back up.

"Why are you asking about them? He said he called you. Why? Are you friends with him? What did he say to you?"

Olivia shook her head, clearly confused.

"Just that something was wrong and you needed me."

Jenna stared at the steam that rose from her tea. She was pissed as tears formed in her eyes. How could one person cry so much? She should be dry and empty.

Olivia gently wrapped her arm around Jenna and scooted over.

"Jen, talk to me?"

"I don't know. I woke up this morning to Julius and the baby... Jax. I don't know who they are. I don't remember anything. He said we're married and Jaxon is mine. But it's not true. I'd never just marry some guy and... Olivia, tell me he's lying. It's not true. He drugged me or this is some weird simulation or...." Tears streamed down her face and splashed in her tea. She continued to babble becoming unintelligible.

Olivia's face sank. She moved to the floor in front of Jenna.

"Jen, look at me."

Jenna raised her head and stared into Olivia's grey eyes.

"Baby, this is real. Julius and Jax. You guys hit it off

and got married two months after you met. And Jax was the perfect pregnancy."

Jenna trembled as her fear overtook her. She lost her grip and the cup slipped from her hand. Olivia jerked back as the glass hit the floor and shattered.

* * *

Hours, days could have passed, Jenna didn't know and didn't care. She lied curled up on the couch. She picked at a string from the woven fabric. What a metaphor. She once was whole now her life was unraveling. Jenna had expected Olivia to give her some peace. Instead, any chance at normalcy had passed. Now her so-called husband and best friend were huddled in the corner, whispering and deciding her fate. Surely a mental institution was on the list. Jenna hated hospitals and doctors. They've never been much use to her. They couldn't save her parents after their accident.

What could they do for her? She wished she could go back, get her life back. No... that wasn't right; she wished she could remember. A soft cooing seeped into Jenna's inner monologue. She peered over the couch.

Jaxon reached up for a colorful rattle that hung from his car seat handle. Jaxon caught a glimpse of Jenna and looked up at her.

"Mom, want to play peek."

Jenna moved back. She realized how stupid she was for hiding from a baby. She moved back to the edge of the couch. Jaxon must've thought she was playing peek-a-boo. He did say play peek. They must've done this a million times.

Jax eyes dilated waiting for Jenna to disappear.

"Peek-a-boo."

Jenna's life may have been in chaos but she couldn't disappoint him. She moved closer to the edge and covered her face with her hands over and over again.

***

Jaxon's laughter filled the air.

"Funny mommy." he loved this game. He knew Jenna hadn't disappeared. But it was still funny to watch her make all those silly faces. Julius stopped mid-sentence. Jaxon only laughed like that with Jenna. His panic receded as he watched the two play peek-a-boo. He was scared for Jenna, for him, but mostly for Jaxon. His dad raised him and he'd always felt something was missing. He had been terrified that that might be his son's fate as well. But watching the two of them now he was hopeful that no matter what the future held Jaxon would have a mother even if he wouldn't have a wife. Julius moved to the kitchen table and dropped his head. He never really considered his life without Jenna. A wave of nausea swept over him.

* * *

The rain had stooped but the waterworks were still flooding Olivia's apartment. Olivia pulled Jaxon from his car seat to offer herself some comfort. The interruption of the game did not make Jaxon happy. He reached out to Jenna and cried. Olivia bounced him on her shoulder and he soon calmed. Olivia looked from her best friend to the broken man sitting at the table. Their family was falling apart in front of her.

"I can't imagine what this is like for either of you. But there aren't any answers here," she said. Olivia laid a sleeping Jax back in his car seat. She sat next to Jenna and pulled her up.

"I know you're scared but you need to go to the hospital."

Jenna nodded, no matter how much she hated

hospitals it was her only option.

* * *

Jenna sat on an exam table in a paper gown. She fiddled with her phone hoping that muscle memory would kick in and she'd remember her password. Right now she wished she hadn't been such a technophobe. The thought of using your fingerprint or face to unlock your phone made her nervous. The rapping on the door brought her back to her unwelcome reality. A tall man wheeled in a cart with vials and needles. Blood work. She cringed. Had she been a wimp when she was pregnant? Jenna held out her arm and turned away. This was the last day of tests, in what had been a two week marathon of poking and prodding. Jenna had visits with six specialists. From virologist to neurologist.

Jenna detached; it was the only way she could cope.

Olivia and Julius waited in the waiting room. She didn't need their concerned looks. Their presence brought her little peace. Jenna's initial visit to the emergency room was consumed with terror. After speaking with the third doctor she realized just how long the road to a diagnosis would be. And even if the cause was discovered there was little chance that it meant a recovery of any of her memories. The mind was still a mystery, they said. The nurse filled up his fourth vial and taped gauze over the puncture.

"I'll be back in a few to take you over to your next test."

Jenna forced a smile. "Thanks."

* * *

Minutes later he returned with a wheelchair and a clipboard of forms. Jenna quickly made her way through the forms. She hesitated at the checkbox asking had she been pregnant. She checked it and wondered if there were any other medical information that she was missing because of her memory loss. Once she was finished she got into the wheelchair and he began pushing her to another part of the hospital.

They passed under one fluorescent light after another. The white on white made the hall seem never-ending. The nurse took the next right and wheeled her into the room at the end of the hall. A large machine with a narrow table and ring filled up most of the space. A small room sat off to the side. Jenna hopped up on the table. The thin paper separating Jenna from the table did little to shield her from the cold.

"Please stay still. The ring is going to move down and scan you now."

It was a red-headed woman that spoke. Her voice was low and monotone, comforting. Jenna exhaled. The ring behind her illuminated. Moving at a snail's pace, the ring inched its way over her body. Jenna closed her eyes, trying to conjure up happier times. She and Olivia moving into their first apartment. The last Christmas with her parents. Jax, his sweet little face. It had been some time since her memory faded away. While she avoided Julius, not sure how to deal with what they were, somehow her relationship with Jax was easy. She figured one never forgot how to be a mom. It was innate in one who'd given birth, even if she couldn't recall any of it.

"Jenna, the test is complete. You can sit up. Someone will be in shortly to take you to your next test."

* * *

Jenna chewed on her nails. Julius and Olivia sat on either side of her. Doctor Greyson had just taken her seat.

Jenna wondered if her slight stature made dispensing bad news easier for patients to handle. Doctor Greyson studied the test results in front of her. Several minutes passed before she met Jenna's gaze.

"I'm so sorry," Doctor Greyson said as she passed a file to Jenna.

Doctor Greyson retuned to reviewing Jenna's test.

"What's this?"

Jenna opened the file and flipped through it. Her pupils dilated and tears filled her eyes. She shook her head.

"I was pregnant."

Doctor Greyson nodded,

"Yes, Jaxon is your son. That is your file, everything from your first appointment with the Obstetrician to your release four days after a natural delivery."

Olivia squeezed Jenna's hand.

"And the other test?"

Doctor Greyson turned her attention back to the eager faces before her.

"Yes, I had hoped something would give us a definitive answer or some clue. But there is not any indication as to why you can't remember the past year. There's no neurological damage, trace of virus, bacteria, or environmental reason that would cause something like this to happen."

"But she is healthy?" Julius asked.

"Yes, Jenna you are the healthiest person I've ever met. Perfect in fact."

"Will I get my memories back?"

"Honestly, I can't say. But I don't want you to misunderstand what I am saying. Just to be clear, you are physically healthy. This doesn't mean you are mentally. Several psychological conditions could be the cause of this mystery."

"I'm not crazy."

"Crazy isn't a medical term. What I mean is, things like stress and other mental conditions, although rare, have been known to cause people to lose their memory."

"Your medical opinion is that I was stressed out?"

Julius placed his hand on top of Jenna's.

"It's okay."

Jenna jerked her hand away.

"No, it's not. She's telling me life made me lose a year."

"I am, in a way. A new marriage and baby is a lot. We all deal with stress differently. And for some people overwhelming stress is a cue to the brain to reboot to a time when everything was working optimally."

Olivia leaned forward.

"What's to stop this from happening again?"

"Nothing, but this is so rare. The odds of it happening again are a trillion to one. I really am sorry, Jenna. I wish we had something concrete to give you.

The best advice I can offer is to live your life and try to find a healthy way to manage your stress. You will need to lean on your family and friends. If anyone notices the slightest change in behavior you should check in just to be safe. At least for the next year.”

Doctor Greyson, moved around her desk and handed Jenna a card.

“If stress is the cause, Doctor Chu can help you. This is a lot. Please take all the time you need.”

Doctor Greyson made her way to the door and shut it behind her.

That was the brilliant doctor’s non-diagnosis and orders. An odd mix of exhaustion and emptiness filled Jenna. Manage her stress. How could she do that with nothing? Block it out. Move forward.

Olivia took the card from Jenna.

“We can deal with this later.”

Jenna released the card. Move forward.

"Hey, O, I need to talk to Julius, alone."

"Sure." Olivia slid her chair back. "Jenna, don't make any decisions. Not right now." Olivia pulled the door shut behind her.

Julius sat up and turned his chair to Jenna's.

"I know it's not much solace but you're okay, healthy."

"Thank you, I know you mean it. I want to be a part of Jaxon's life, but I just don't know how to process us."

"Yeah, I get it. But I'm here for you."

"I know." Jenna leaned over and kissed Julius on his cheek.

***

Jenna flitted about the living room. She gathered Jaxon's toys and stuffed them in a diaper bag. It had been almost a month since she woke up in this upside-down world. She was still getting used to being in such close proximity to Julius but she was thankful that Olivia had temporally moved in to be a buffer. Jenna knew the new arrangement had been hard on Julius. But it was the only thing she could think of that allowed her to get to know Jaxon while putting some clear distance between her and her husband. Gosh, the word still felt off even in her head. It carried with it such a heavy obligation and there was no way she was ready to deal with it. Although Julius never voiced it she could tell he was waiting for her to come around.

"Olivia, have you seen Jax's teething ring?" Jenna asked as she turned her search to the refrigerator, sink, and counters.

Olivia hopped out of the spare bedroom with one shoe in hand.

"Try the couch. Where is the brat anyway?" Olivia slipped her shoe on and made her way to the kitchen.

She filled a cup with coffee and sat at the table.

Jenna rushed to the couch. She dug between the cushions and pulled out the teething ring. "Still sleeping."

"So, you do remember that I'm headed out of town for the weekend? Right?"

"Yes." Jenna rinsed off the teething ring and stuffed it in the bag. "Don't do anything stupid, I need you back in one piece."

Olivia exhaled and jumped from her seat.

"I wanted to talk to you about that." Olivia placed her hands on her hips and stared at Jenna.

"What's wrong?" Jenna stiffened. She prepared herself for bad news hoping that no matter what it was that it could be fixed.

"I love you, but I can't continue staying here. You gotta know you're safe. This is where you belong and me being here is just preventing you from dealing with

194

the elephant in the room."

Jenna's heart raced, she could hear her blood pumping in her ears. This wasn't the end of the world. It was just another change. She could handle this and, of course, Olivia was right. She had asked way too much of her bestie and Olivia had come through for her. Jenna let a smile spread across her face as she thought of how grateful she was to have Olivia. Jenna threw her arms around the woman. "Thank you for everything."

"I'm still here, you know."

Jenna bobbed her head up and down.

"Hey, what's that?" Olivia pulled a phone out of Jenna's back pocket.

"I was going to take it to the wireless store to see if they could get me in it."

Olivia tapped a few keys and the screen lit up. A picture of Jenna, Julius, and a newborn Jaxon between them filled the screen. Olivia held the phone out to show

Jenna.

"You guys are so cute. You were excited."

Jenna stared at the phone in awe. She snatched the phone from Olivia. Jenna swiped through the apps until she found the photo app. With one click all her forgotten family memories were accessible. Pictures and videos of her and Julius in love. Jenna played a video of Julius singing to her belly. Them decorating the nursery. Jenna plopped on the couch.

"It's all here. The whole year. How did you know the password?

"It's the date you guys met. You said it was the day that changed your life."

"Sappy."

Olivia hugged Jenna.

"See you later. Tell Julius I said bye."

"Yeah, have a good day."

"I'm sure you will." Olivia finished her coffee.

"What does that mean?"

"You two are finally going to be alone. That man is amazing and based on everything you told me about him you loved everything about him. Take this weekend to get to know him before someone snatches him up." Olivia grabbed her purse and keys and left.

Jenna sat on her bed. She looked down on a sleeping Jaxon. She held the phone with a photo of Julius up to Jaxon. He looked like Julius around the eyes. Jenna watched a video of Julius feeding Jaxon, then one of them playing. She could feel the tears forming. She stuffed the phone in her pocket.

Jenna wasn't going to get all gooey over the man she saw on her phone. That was one version of him. She hadn't spent much time with him. But those were the videos she had chosen to capture. That was the Julius she had wanted to remember. Jenna hadn't wanted to face it but everyone went on and on about how great Julius was. Especially

Olivia. It was obvious he was a great dad and he loved her.
He was being patient with her. She knew she was being
unfair. Their marriage needed to be addressed. No matter
what, they were Jax's parents. Olivia was right. She needed
to get to know Julius.

Maybe they could be friends. With benefits. Jenna
shook her head. Where had that thought come from? She
only had one look at him that day she woke up. She had
dreamt of him on more than one occasion. No. No. She
wasn't doing this. Friends. That was it. She'd talk to Julius
tonight and discuss moving forward. Great. This was great.
Jenna pulled on Jaxon's jacket. He wined at the annoyance
but held back cries. She gently picked Jaxon up and
situated him in his stroller.

* * *

Playtime with Jaxon was a full body workout. She held

onto his hand. It was amazing at only a few months old that he was walking as if he were a toddler. Jax pulled away from her. He was a runner and she knew if she let go of him for a minute he would take off. Just yesterday he got to the other side of the park within a minute. It was probably best to just minimize the risk. Jenna picked Jaxon up and adjusted him on her hip. She pulled on the door but it was locked. Weird. Julius was home, his car was in the driveway. He usually left it unlocked. Jenna dug into her pocket. Where were her keys? Had Jaxon grown since this morning? Maybe they should cut back on the oatmeal. Jenna moved him to the other arm. She dug into the purse that was slung over her shoulder. How could she lose her keys? She beat on the door with her newly freed hand with urgency. Where was he? She could call him but that felt weird. Jenna returned to her purse.

"Keys, mommy?" Jaxon said, shaking the keys and laughing.

She exhaled. This kid of hers was a prankster among other things. "What's mommy going to do with you?"

* * *

Jenna tucked Jaxon in his crib. She watched his chest rise and fall. A smile tugged at the corners of her mouth. A fragrant scent wafted in from the kitchen. There was food on. Where was Julius? She turned on the baby monitor and pulled the door shut. With the other half of the monitor in hand she made her way to the kitchen to find no Julius but several pots on the stove; one boiling over.

She sat the monitor on the counter and turned the burner down. Whatever he was cooking looked great. The smell filled her nose as she stared at the food. There was chicken thawing in the sink. She decided to cut the chicken. She seasoned it and added it to the concoction in the pot. Julius rounded the corner in sweats. He smiled at her then asked,

"Jaxon?"

"Asleep." Jenna held the baby monitor out to Julius.

"I've got him the rest of the night."

"We can tag team it. Umm, I did want to talk to you," she said.

"How about now? Over dinner."

"I'm assuming you were making chicken stew."

"Yeah, your recipe. I'll get cleaned up." Julius turned back down the hall.

Was this what it was like before? No, he was charming, that was clear, but this time he was cheating. He knew everything about her. And he had Olivia in his corner. There was no need to make this more awkward. Honestly, she wasn't sure she could really handle being alone with him. Not after seeing how they were together. She couldn't be sure if she felt something or if this was all in her head. She had to be sure since Olivia was no longer around to be a buffer. Jenna opened the freezer and swung the door back and forth. The artificial breeze relaxed her. Food, peace, bed. Food, peace, bed. Okay, she could do this.

* * *

Jenna was astonished as she watched Julius dig into his food. He consumed with enthusiasm yet savored every bite. Her mind wondered. She could imagine their lips pressed together. His hand on her neck. His chest pressed against hers. Jenna scratched her ear and cleared her throat. Water. Jenna snatched up her glass and gulped down the contents.

Julius smirked.

"Sorry, you wanted to talk."

Jenna wiped her mouth.

"Umm, yes. So, we're married..."

"Yes." Julius didn't miss a beat bringing food to his

mouth.

"I think it's time we get to know each other. For Jaxon. We should know each other better."

Julius set his fork down and wiped his mouth.

"I know you. I can tell you're anxious. I know you want to kiss me and..."

"Okay, you know me." she responded.

"You are thinking too much."

"Last year is gone. Everyone remembers it but me. I like how things are, but I don't want to be unfair to you. You have to understand all this is new to me. You're great, but I need for us to be friends."

Julius grimaced.

"You know we were never friends."

"Maybe that's the problem. I can't believe I'd get involved with anyone seriously after such a short time. It's not me."

"Maybe you should try it."

"Julius, don't make this harder."

"Jenna you're the only one putting pressure on this.
You want to be friends, I'll be your best friend. You
want to be lovers, kiss me. You want to be my wife, say
it. I love you. I'm here any way you want me."

A tingle ran down Jenna's spine. He was serious.
Worse yet he was right. The ball was in her court and
had always been.

"Right now I just want answers."

Julius leaned back and crossed his arms.

"Ask."

It was that simple, wasn't it? All her answers had
been with Julius the whole time.

"I was finally able to get in my old phone. I watched
the videos. We were happy."

"We were. We can be again."

"I don't know if I'm her. How did we get together?"

"I don't remember really. But I do remember waking

up the next morning watching you sleep. I guess we drank too much. But I was in awe of you. And I knew none of it made sense but you and me, we did."

"So you woke up and figured, why not?"

"I did. You know you were the first woman I brought back here. I figured you had to be worth it if we ended up in that bed."

"So you're not against one night stands just as long as it's her house and you can take off."

The table shook with Julius's laughter. "That's why I love you. Cutting straight through the crap."

"Why did I love you?"

"You said I felt like home, someone you could build a family with. Olivia was all you had after your parents and even if we never had kids you had a family again."

Jenna trembled. Family. That had been her wish since her parents' death. She wanted a deep connection with someone. That was what truly terrified her since she woke that day. She had been afraid that she'd lost that dream again. And she wasn't willing to go through all that pain a third time. Maybe this was what Doctor Greyson had been talking about. She hadn't dealt with her parents' death. Maybe that fear of losing Julius and Jaxon had been too much and she broke. You can't lose what you don't remember.

Julius leaned over and gently kissed Jenna. She jerked away, tears spilling down her face.

"Just to clarify that wasn't sexual."

Maybe not, but it did snap Jenna out of her spiral.

"You got anything stronger?"

"Wine or Jack."

"Jack!"

"That's my girl." Julius pulled down the Jack Daniels and two glasses. He filled the glasses and held his up to Jenna.

Jenna tapped her glass against Julius's.

"To good health and fewer tears."

Jenna threw back her drink and winked at Julius, challenging him to follow suit. Julius took his drink in a gulp. He refilled both cups and nodded to Jenna.

* * *

Jenna and Julius sat across from each other with an empty bottle between them. Their laughter echoed throughout the room. She leaned to the right as she rose from her seat. She stumbled to the door. Julius watched her, confused.

"Where do you think you're going?" Julius grabbed her arm and pulled her into him.

Jenna pulled away.

"I need some air. I feel woozy."

"Because you're drunk." Julius lifted Jenna and carried her down the hallway.

Jenna gulped. She avoided his gaze.

"Don't worry, I'm taking you to your room," he reassured her.

Julius rounded the corner and tripped over a rattle. He and Jenna tumbled into the bed.

"This is you being a gentleman?"

For a second they just watched each other, before Julius peeled himself off the bed.

"I'll see you in the morning."

Jenna jumped out of the bed and tackled Julius. He turned toward her and lost his composure. Jenna sank into Julius's kisses.

"I'm starting to get your appeal."

"We don't have to rush," he told her.

Jenna smiled up at him. "I know." She pulled him closer. She caressed his face and smiled.

* * *

Streaks of morning light softened as they passed through the thin gossamer curtain. The golden flecks in Jenna's tan skin caught the light as she stretched. Jenna rolled over. She yawned with each stretch. She sat herself up on her elbows and watched Julius's eyes flutter. She snuggled in closer to him. She wouldn't forget this time. She'd write it all down just in case. She pulled on his shirt and ran out of the room. She peered in Jaxon's room. He was sleeping as soundly as his dad. She found her purse on the couch in the living room. She pulled the phone from her purse and turned to return to bed. She bumped into a hard mass.

Julius stood before her terrified.

"Are you okay?" Julius pulled Jenna close. "Do you know who I am?"

"Julius, you're smothering me. I should be asking you if you remember me."

Julius loosened his grip but kept Jenna pressed to his chest.

"I thought you left."

"No, I remember. I just wanted to start a diary."

Julius lead Jenna down the hallway.

"You get in bed. I'll cook us some breakfast and take care of Jaxon."

"He's fine. I checked on him before I got this." Jenna waved her phone in the air.

Julius smacked Jenna's butt.

"Okay, back to bed."

Jenna jumped.

"Only cause I'm hungry, caveman."

Jenna settled in bed with her phone. She dialed Olivia but it went straight to voicemail. "Hey, I just wanted to let you know, you were right. I think I'm gonna try this wife thing. See how it goes. I'll talk to you later. And, O, thanks for everything."

Jenna sank into the bed. She swiped through her apps and opened the diary. The diary opened to the last entry. It was dated the night before Jenna lost her memory. The words Jenna read shocked her. *Everything is okay. Read every entry. Everything you need and want to know is here.* Jenna scrolled to the first entry. It was a chronicle of her lost time. Jenna tapped on the first entry. It went on and on about Julius being the perfect man and how she knew their child would be perfect. Jenna felt like she was reading someone else's words. In many ways, it was juvenile, like a lovesick teenager. What made her think she and Julius would get together much less last and become parents? The more Jenna read the weirder the entries became. There were notes on how to properly take care of Jaxon and preparing him for life without his other half. Was she losing her mind? Is that what really happened, was this the real answer? Doctor Greyson had said there were conditions that could cause memory loss, but Jenna never considered that a real possibility.

Julius entered with a tray of food.

"Time to eat, sexy."

Jenna felt like she aged ten years since opening the diary.

"I kept a diary." Jenna held the phone out to him.

Julius braced himself. He didn't want to take it. But the panic in Jenna's face told him he had too. He skimmed entry after entry. Ten minutes later he caressed Jenna's hands.

"Look at me. This means nothing, other than you were a good mom. You wanted to make sure he was taken care of no matter what."

"And if it means something else?"

"We'll deal with it."

Jenna threw her arms around Julius. He crawled into bed and they ate and talked. Jaxon barely made a peep as if he knew they needed the time to work things out.

It turned out to be the beginning of a new tradition.
Jenna added to the diary each day and Saturdays became
their favorite day. They took turns cooking breakfast in
bed for the other. They talked and spent those mornings
in bed wrapped in one another's arms.

* * *

December 26, 2009br

An unusually fit nine-year-old Jaxon gripped the
handlebars of his bike. His two best friends Pete, a slender
boy, and Sadia, a skinny girl, followed close behind. They
raced through the neighborhood on their brand new bikes.
Christmas had been good to them all this year. Jaxon sped
down the street and hopped his bike on the sidewalk. Pete
copied the move. The two boys looked back at Sadia. Sadia
shook her head and followed alongside her friends in the

street. Jaxon stretched out his arms and closed his eyes.

"Heads up," Sadia huffed.

Jaxon opened his eyes in time to see a Frisbee fly past. Jaxon slammed on his breaks. He stopped as a small kid ran past.

"That was close."

Jaxon swung his bike off the sidewalk. He leaned to the right and the others followed him downtown. The edge of the town was at the top of a steep hill. This was the reason they biked rather than walking or getting a ride. The thrill of soaring down that hill made you feel like you were flying. Jaxon and his friends had plenty of places to play in their small town but downtown was where all the real fun was. There were shops, skate parks, and plenty of opportunities for them to get in trouble. Jaxon nodded to his friends and closed his eyes. He smiled and leaned forward. Jaxon and his bike careened down the hill.

* * *

They slowed down and hopped off their bikes. A few feet away was their hangout; it was better than any clubhouse. The neon open sign blinked in the window. They rolled their bikes to the side of the building and parked them in the bike rack. They ran around the corner. Their faces lit up like it was Christmas all over. A bell rang above the door as the group entered.

Arcade games, foosball tables, and an assortment of flashing games filled the space. A bald man leaned on the counter. He puffed on his cigar and waved them in. The friends look around the full arcade. Kids rushed from one game to another. They formed lines at the most popular games, lining their tokens up on the side of the arcade games. They pushed their way through the crowd to the coin machine and fed it ten dollars. Coins spilled out the bottom of the machine, Pete scraped them into a bucket.

"I told you we should have come earlier. The new games all have lines."

Sadia stuck her tongue out at Pete.

"I can't help that my grandma won't let me out of the house before ten."

Pete rolled his eyes.

"Next time we're leaving without you."

"But she won't let me go by myself," Sadia fired back.

Jaxon stepped between the two.

"It doesn't matter. We'll play something else while we wait."

Sadia smirked at Pete. Pete shook his head.

"Whatever."

They ran off in different directions looking for games with no lines. Pete waved his hand about.

"I found one. Over here."

Sadia and Jaxon rushed to his side. Their faces dropped at the sight of a princess racing game.

"This is not a game, Pete," Jaxon said as he rolled his eyes.

"Did either of you find anything?" Pete glared at his friends, clearly annoyed. Jaxon and Sadia shook their heads.

"Okay then let's play or go home."

Sadia shrugged.

"Maybe something else will open up soon."

Pete grabbed a coin out of the bucket and dropped it in the slot.

"Imma play." Pete sat at the game and picked the Grape Princess. Three. Two. One. The flag dropped and Pete slammed his foot on the pedal. A smile spread across Pete's face as he yanked the wheel to the left bumping the Strawberry Princess off the track.

"Gotcha."

Jaxon and Sadia cheered Pete on as he bumped one princess car after another one off the track. But Orange Marmalade maintained her lead by zig-zagging across the track.

"Oh no you don't!"

Pete matched her movements. He zigged when she zagged and took the lead. Grape Princess crossed the finish line. Grape Princess leapt in the air. Crystal Princess floated down to the track and placed a crown atop Grape Princess's head. Fireworks shot into the pastel sky. Pete turned to his friends.

"Think you two can do better?"

Sadia dropped a coin in the slot and hit the player two button.

"Let's go, Princess."

The countdown began. Three. Two. One. Sadia and Pete slammed their feet on the pedal knocking princesses off the track one by one, till Grape Princess and

Pineapple Princess were the only two left in the race.
The two friends slammed their princess cars into each
other causing them both to spin out. They regained
control and the screen went blank.

Pete jumped out of his seat.

"What happened?"

A large boy swung the plug to the game in his hand.

"Nice racing, ladies."

Pete slid out of his seat.

"You owe us a game," Pete said as he held his hand
out.

"Sorry, I'm all out." The boy dropped the cord. He
turned around and chuckled.

"Hey everyone, check out the girls in the back at the
princess game."

Pete launched himself at the boy. They fell to the ground
and wrestled. A crowd gathered around them as they
traded punches. A group of adults cleared a path through

the jeering kids. They pulled Pete and the boy apart. A man with curly red hair held the boy by the collar.

"Who started this?"

"He unplugged our game," Sadia spoke up.

"You're always picking a fight. I'm too old for this. Get out and don't come back."

"I didn't do anything."

"Yeah, yeah. Tell your momma. Now, get out."

The boy shrugged away from the red headed man.

"I'll see you, babies, outside." The bell rang as the boy slunk out the door and jogged across the street.

"Nothing more to see here. Go play."

The kids murmured to each other as they made their way back to the games. Jaxon plugged the game back in.

"You want to play again?" Jaxon held a token out to Pete.

Pete shook his head.

"Let's just go home."

"We just got here."

"You two my momma now?" Pete pushed his way to the front door and exited the arcade.

A confused Jaxon and Sadia followed after Pete.

"You won the fight. Why are you mad?" Sadia asked.

Pete walked to the side of the building to find the bike rack empty.

"Where's my bike?"

Jaxon and Sadia rushed to the rack.

"My grandma's gonna kill me," Sadia said, starting to hyperventilate.

Jaxon patted Sadia on the back.

"If you don't calm down you'll die before she has a chance."

"Hello, babies!"

They all turned to look. The bully from the arcade stood at the end of the alley with a stick in hand. All three of their bikes were next to him. He kicked at Sadia's bike.

"Do the babies want their bikes back?"

Sadia shivered.

"Let's just go get someone from the arcade."

Pete shook his head.

"No, we can take him. It's three to one."

The boy raised the stick and brought it down hard on Pete's bike.

"What the babies gonna do?"

Pete took off with Jaxon close on his heels. Sadia huffed as she followed after her friends. Pete tackled the boy. They boy swung the stick and hit Pete in the leg. Jaxon crouched and waited for an opening. The boy threw the stick. It smacked Sadia in the head. Sadia grabbed her head and staggered back. The boy fell back laughing.

"Look poor baby's hurt." The boy looked at Jaxon.

"You think you got something, kid? Come at me if you

wanna fight." The boy waved Jaxon over.

Jaxon looked back at his friend. His eyes flashed in

anger, he leapt in the air and came down on the boy. The

boy crashed into the concrete. Jaxon straddled him. He

swung his left fist then his right, left, right, left, right.

The boys friends ran in fear. Jaxon continued to punched

the boy over and over again. The boy reached around for

something to defend himself with. Finally, he found a

bottle and cracked it over Jaxon's head. The glass

shattered and for a second Jaxon lost his focus. He

pulled his arm back and swung but something stopped

him just before his fist slammed into the boy's face.

Jaxon jerked back and stared at the boy's bloody

face. Jaxon pulled Sadia and Pete to their feet. They each

grabbed their bikes and wheeled them toward the street.

Sensing something, Jaxon turned around to find the boy

and his wrecked face running toward them. He tripped

and fell to the ground and cried out.

Jaxon and Pete looked back in awe.

"We better get out of here before someone comes," Pete said.

They hopped on their bikes and sped off.

"Hey, Jaxon your head okay?" Sadia asked.

"Yeah."

"He cracked a bottle over your head."

Jaxon reached up and gently surveyed his head with his hand. He plucked several shards from his hair and shrugged.

"It's fine, my mom says I have a hard head."

"I don't think that's what it means, Superman."

"Superman?"

"Yeah, you gotta be the man of steel, Me and Pete are all bruised and you acting like a bottle to the head was just some plastic toy."

Jaxon shrugged. They continued down the street

enjoying their victory.

* * *

Jenna smoothed her towel across the pool chair. She wiggled around until she found the right position. Julius and Jaxon splashed each other in the shallow end of the pool. Jaxon's smile faded as he scanned the community pool.

"Where's everybody?" Jaxon asked.

"Learn to enjoy quiet moments. If this place was packed you'd never get a chance to just enjoy the water."

Jaxon shrugged.

"I still wish the guys were here," he said.

Julius pulled himself out of the pool and grabbed the football by Jenna's chair.

"Ready?"

Jaxon raised his hand and prepared himself. Julius

threw the ball in the air. Jaxon pushed himself off the bottom of the pool and with explosive force he launched himself out of the pool. Jaxon reached up. His fingers wrapped around the ball. Julius's eyes widened in awe of his son's accomplishment.

"Jenna, did you see that? Our boy is gonna be a star receiver, the greatest ever. Jax, throw it back. Jenna watch." Julius turned to Jenna.

Jaxon bobbed in the water and hurled the ball back.

"Jenna, you watching?"

Jenna lowered her book and sat up.

"Yes, honey. I'm watching."

Julius turned back to find the football inches away. He moved to raise his hands but the football hit him square in the chest. The force pushed Julius back. He stumbled and hit the ground. Jenna dropped her book and knelt beside Julius.

"You alright?"

Julius coughed as he held his chest. Jaxon sprang from the pool and rushed to Julius's side. "Dad?"

"Why the worried looks guys? I'm good." Julius rubbed his chest.

"This is why you never take your eye off the ball. Help me up."

Jenna and Jaxon pulled Julius to his feet and helped him to a chair.

Jenna patted Jaxon on the shoulder.

"He's fine. I swear he just forgets he's old. Go play."

A group of people made their way in and filled up the seats by the pool. Kids cannonballed into the pool. Jaxon sat on the chair next to Julius.

"See, bet you wish it was just us again," Julius said.

Jaxon didn't answer. He just stared at Julius, concerned.

"I'm good, promise. Go play," Julius urged.

Jaxon patted Julius on the leg. He ran off and cannonballed into the pool. Julius watched Jaxon splash the other kids.

"Kid's strong."

"You sure you're fine?" Jenna asked as she rubbed Julius's chest.

Julius winced. "Yeah, just bruised. But I don't mind having your hands all over me."

Julius leaned back. Jenna moved back to her seat and laid back.

* * *

The sun beamed down on a sleeping Jenna. She shielded her eyes as she sat up. Julius snored beside her. Jenna scanned the area. She shook Julius's shoulder.

"Hey, wake up. We can sleep at home."

Julius waved his hand, clearly annoyed at the

interruption.

"Come on," Jenna said as she continued searching. "I don't see Jaxon."

"Of course not. There's probably a million kids in the pool now."

Jenna stood and moved closer to the pool. "Jaxon? Time to go."

Jenna moved around the pool quickly then returned to her husband.

"Julius, I don't see him."

Julius rubbed the sleep from his eyes. He briefly massaged his chest and rose from the chair.

"Relax, I'll check the bathroom," Julius said as he made his way to the back where the bathrooms and showers were.

Jenna saw a group of kids gathered around the deep end of the pool. A small boy gripped a stopwatch.

"Six minutes!" he shouted excited.

A towering girl pushed the boy over and yanked the stopwatch away.

"No way, you're lying."

The group cheered. Jenna moved closer to the rowdy kids and pulled a young girl to her. "What's going on?" she asked.

"I think he's dead."

"Who?" Jenna asked, anxiety knifing through her.

The girl frowned at Jenna and pulled away from her.

"A boy's down there, holding his breath."

Jenna pushed through the crowd. The kids groaned at Jenna's intrusion.

"Eight minutes," one kid screamed.

Jenna dropped to her knees and gasped.

"Jaxon? Julius! Julius..."

Jaxon sat at the bottom of the pool. Tiny bubbles escaped his mouth and floated to the surface. Jaxon stared at his reflection.

"How long do you think we can last?"

"Let's see," his reflection responded.

Panic griped Jenna. She dropped into the water and dove down to Jaxon. Jaxon smiled and waved at his mother. Jenna reached out and yanked Jaxon up from the bottom. She kicked hard, propelling them both upward. They emerged, breaking the surface of the water.

Julius ran forward and pulled his wife and son from the pool.

"What the hell happened?"

Kids surrounded Jaxon. They patted him on the back.

"Wow."

"That was amazing."

Julius pushed the kids away. "Give us some space."

Annoyed, the kids jumped in the pool.

Jenna lied on the ground huffing.

"What were you doing, Jaxon?"

"Wasn't it cool? Do you know how long I held my

breath?" Jaxon jumped up and ran to the boy with the stopwatch.

"Let me see. Ten minutes and thirty-five seconds."

Jenna and Julius watched Jaxon with a mix of awe and confusion.

Julius pulled Jenna to her feet.

"Someone tell me what happened."

"He was holding his breath. He could have died," Jenna panted.

"Jenna, he's fine."

Jenna shook her head.

"We're going home."

"Yeah okay. I'll get Jaxon."

Julius waved Jaxon over.

The adoring crowd high fived Jaxon as Jenna stuffed their items in her bag.

Jaxon broke away from the crowd and ran to his father.

"But I don't wanna go. I was just starting to have fun."

"No, we're leaving, now. You scared the crap outta me," Jenna said, her voice trembling.

"I was just playing."

"I don't care, we're leaving."

"Sorry, buddy. It's been a long day," Julius said as he patted Jaxon on the back.

Jenna stuffed the towel in her bag and strutted toward the gates.

Julius and Jaxon trailed behind. After a few seconds Julius stopped Jaxon.

"You're too much of a show-off. You can't go around scaring your mom like that, man. Okay?"

Jaxon looked back at his fans and then slowly nodded.

* * *

A fourteen-year-old Jaxon and Pete pumped their legs hard and fast. The two boys turned down the side street and behind a shopping center. Jaxon pulled ahead of Pete.

"Wait up!" Pete shouted as he looked back over his shoulder at the snarling pit-bull.

"Run faster!" Jaxon screamed. "This is your fault, you just had to throw the rock."

Pete's chest heaved. His muscles contracted as he slowed. The pit-bull leapt forward. He snapped his jaws inches away from Pete's leg. Pete screamed and a burst of adrenaline pushed him forward. He gained speed and caught up with Jaxon.

"Superman, why don't you just take care of it?"

Jaxon smirked at his friend. "Why should I?"

"Come on man. I don't want to be eaten."

Jaxon shook his head. "You owe me Pete."

***

Jaxon stopped and turned toward the dog. Pete continued on. Jaxon looked back over his shoulder. He watched Pete stumble up a hill that separated the stores from the apartment complex above. Jaxon threw his arms up.

"If I get hurt. I'm blaming you."

"Best seat in the house. You got thi..."

The pit-bull used its hind legs to spring into the air. It opened its jaws wide and clamped down on Jaxon's arm. Jaxon shook his arm wildly. The dog growled and clung to Jaxon's arm. Jaxon grimaced. He had been stupid to think he could really take on a pit.

We can.

Jaxon swung his arm and flung the pit-bull to the ground. It crouched low and bared its teeth as it growled at him. Jaxon followed suit and got low, matching movements with the dog. He searched the area for some kind of weapon. He saw a chain wrapped around the trunk of a tree off to the side. Jaxon jumped past the pit-bull and grabbed the chain. The pit-bull leapt into the air and came down hard on Jaxon's chest knocking him to the ground. Jaxon wrapped his arm around the pit-bull's neck. The pit-bull snarled.

"Come on, Superman, you got him."

Drool dripped on Jaxon's face.

"A little help would be nice."

Jaxon wrestled the animal. He used his free arm to connect the chain to the collar on the pit-bull. He was finally able to push the dog off of him into the side of the tree. The dog yelped. Jaxon rolled out of reach of the chain and hobbled off. Coming down from his adrenaline rush, Jaxon fell to the ground and lied on his back, staring up at the sky.

Pete slid down the hill and rushed to his friend. He stared down at Jaxon.

"What I tell you? Superman always wins."

"Until he was killed."

Jaxon rolled over. He wiped the dirt off his clothes as he made his way to his feet.

Pete patted Jaxon on the back.

"I'm tired of that Superman crap. That dog could've torn me apart," Jaxon said.

"It's not like you got hurt."

Jaxon raised his arm.

"What do you call this?" Jaxon rolled his ripped sleeve up. His eyes bulged.

"I don't understand. It bit me."

Pete leaned over to see Jaxon's arm which was unblemished.

"I told you. Nothing can hurt you."

Jaxon rubbed his arm.

"Am I Superman?" A smile spread across Jaxon's face. "I'm Superman."

Pete smacked Jaxon on the back. "Let's find out what else you can do, Superman."

Pete and Jaxon took off up the hill.

What is this fiery chill that prickles the surface of my skin? It seems the shifting celestial orbs have delivered their timely solstice in a mysterious new cloak. A thick, foreboding power—it neither warms nor cools me, rather directs my skin how to feel.

Though in its incipience, already I see it coating the landscape—every branch, twig, and leaf dips under its weight. It comes smothering the horizon, with none of nature's children escaping its might. Indeed, this budding power is wont to consume it all!

My mind is as weak as a flower under its gale force, unable to perceive its dimensions. Colors beyond description, beauty unimaginable—the sight is too extravagant for my eyes to observe though its scale floods my vision.

Look away as I might, it draws my heart back in with its powerful rhythm. From under its dazzling plumage beats a source of energy that sets the ground to tremble beneath my feet.

Its draping sleeves embrace me. My whole body sways under its gentle direction—a carnival of the most marvelous wonders!

Though I sense that if it wanted, this power could enrobe me for the rest of time.

Pray for us all that the shoulders upon which this

powerful garment rests be righteous! This world could dance on its fingertips just as easily as it could die by its fists.

Such a coup of nature's stability would require an element unlike any other—neither fire nor ice, nor force of wind—yet I sense this cloak and its bearer could overpower them all. In truth, they could grow to do far worse.

Though must I jump to the darkest of suspicions? Surely a rational explanation exists for this disruption that my mind has yet to comprehend. Closure to my mind requires bringing closure to my heart.

I will seek this powerful cloak-wearer for my answers. It has been too long since I've held him, and the need has never been more grave.

Chapter 5

Self-reflection

July 24,2018br

6:02AM

The *inner* was not used to being outside of Jaxon's body. Everything felt heightened.

"*How did I end up in this situation?*" he wondered. This was not supposed to happen. "*I'm supposed to be the inner of us, of me.*"

Everything in the world felt new to him. The sounds,

the smells, the sights. The people wandering in the streets, the cars buzzing around, the birds chirping, the squirrels climbing trees and chasing each other. The smell of the air. The flowers. The brightness of the sky.

It's a whole new planet out here.

As time passed, he slowly started to feel elated.

What is this I'm feeling? Euphoria? Ecstasy? Why did it take so long for me to experience this? To experience being alive?

He inhaled, and then let out a deep breath.

I'm alive!

His existence was real. So real. He could hear the beating of his heart, he could feel the blood running in his veins. He took another deep breath, and exhaled. Soothing. He closed his eyes for a second to soak things in. He lifted his head and looked up at the sky, observing the clouds.

I'm alive!

He clenched his fists. He looked at his hands, his fingers. Every detail of his body was so well thought out.

He took more steps. Sounds were all around him. His ears buzzed with car horns, fire trucks, dog barks, baby cries. He covered his ears with his hands.

How can people take all of this in without exploding?

Somehow he found Jaxon at Flower Valley Adventist hospital. He asked the receptionist, a chubby brunette with square rimmed glasses.

"Hello, I'm here to see Jaxon, can you help me?"

She told him he needed to sign in and take the elevator to the 5th floor.

When he stepped in the elevator. He looked down, continuing to check himself out. He saw that he was wearing a 5k T-shirt.

5K? What's a 5K?

Ah, he remembered now. It was a marathon that he didn't want to run with Pete and Sadia. A couple of years ago, Jaxon was not much of a runner, but somehow they

convinced him to do it anyway.

"Running will ruin your knees," his granddad

thought, but Jaxon never listened.

He smiled when he remembered their conversation.

Where did these clothes come from? When did I get

dressed? I don't remember. Some things will remain

unresolved forever, he thought. He ran his fingers across

his face. He felt stubble. Do I need to shave?

He grabbed the eight-point, star necklace around his

neck. A force of energy ran through him. Suddenly, he

felt peace, a sense of warmth. This force somehow

grounded him. He felt a sense of home. He touched it

again as he felt this force run though his veins.

How did he get to the hospital? He had no clue.

Another mystery that would remain unresolved. After

the accident, all he remembered was talking to Pete and

Sadia and feeling really weak, then darkness, and

nothing else. Right before he blacked out, he knew that he needed to help Jaxon.

He wanted to find a way to make things right. He looked at the three other people who shared the elevator ride with him. There was a young man wearing scrubs and two middle-aged women who looked tired and in need of sleep. The elevator was small. With his heightened senses he could smell just about everything, from the anesthesia in the operating room to the candy bar wrapped up in the lady's purse next to him. He could almost taste it. He could even feel the vibrations of the elevator mechanisms working, twisting, and turning.

He looked at the people sharing the elevator with him and thought Can they really tell if I'm different? Do I look like everyone else? Do I smell different? Am I acting different?

To his surprise, no one seemed to notice anything unusual. Everyone seemed to be lost in thought, consumed with the mundanities of their everyday life, checking their phones or staring at the elevator door. He could totally walk this earth unnoticed. Being separated from Jaxon excited him, but was both physically and mentally exhausting. He wanted Jaxon back; he needed to be joined again.

He got out of the elevator and walked toward the end of the hallway to room 503. The omnipresent scene of antiseptic gave him a headache, and he felt nauseated. He stopped, took a deep breath, and then kept walking.

He was going to see Jaxon face-to-face for the first time. He was anxious but also nervous. He'd seen Jaxon's reflection in the mirror all of his life. He knew exactly how he looked.

He still had some fond memories of their childhood, when Jaxon would laugh whenever Jenna placed him in front of the mirror. He would smile, point at the mirror, and say *Baby*. His mother, of course, thought nothing of it. She thought that her baby was just reacting to his own image in the mirror. When he started forming words, he told his mom about the guy in the mirror. His mom also never made anything of it. "All kids have imaginary friends," she told her husband when they discussed their son's behavior in front of the mirror.

When Jaxon grew up, he realized that he was special. That he was the only one in his family and maybe in the world that could actually see the voice in his head and not only hear him. He kept that secret to himself. Nobody would understand, he told himself.

As he approached Jaxon's hospital room, he could hear the beating of his heart, slow but steady.

What a weird feeling. What an exhilarating sensation to be separated.

When he entered the hospital room, he quickly scanned the surroundings. There he was--"Jaxon". He was asleep peacefully in his bed, covered in a thin sheet, with two IV's sticking out of his arm. Next to his bed was a table that had white lilies, a couple of magazines, and a glass of water. Above him on the ceiling was a blinding bright neon light.

His bed was under a huge window that showed the view of the blue mountains, the mountains that Jaxon grew up watching. *What a beautiful sight*, he thought.

Maybe being separate is worth it after all, just for the views.

Even from where he was standing, he could see Jaxon's bruised up face. Bruises under his eyes, on his cheek.

He froze. This was the first time they got separated, and he felt the need to be united again.

How can he make that happen? What does he need to do to be joined again?

"Can I help you? asked Pete interrupting his daze.

The *inner* looked at Pete, Jaxon's friend since

elementary school. He knew Pete really well. He remembered how kids teased Pete for his red hair and called him "ginger" and "rusty hair." He remembered the many times Jaxon defended him, how he stood up to the bullies. He remembered his first heartbreak, and how he cried quietly in Jaxon's room after his crush left him for a guy from the football team. He remembered how happy he was when he got his university acceptance letter, and how he shared the news with Jaxon before he shared it with his own family. He remembered the river of tears Pete shed when he shared the news of his dad's diagnosis, and how elated he was when his dad was officially declared cancer-free. These two were indeed best friends and would remain like that for life.

Pete was sitting in a chair underneath the window. He had his phone in his hand. He looked like he hadn't shaven in days. His white long-sleeved shirt was wrinkled, and he had a big noticeable stain on his brown khaki pants.

Next to him in a chair was a pretty young woman with long, dark hair, brown eyes, and a light complexion "*Sadia*". The three of them, Jaxon, Pete, and Sadia, were inseparable since elementary school. The *inner* was well aware of Sadia's secret crush on Jaxon. She always laughed at his jokes and asked him to help her with her homework. Jaxon was aware of it, but chose not to do anything about it. He was too consumed with his own life, trying to figure out the meaning of it all. The voice inside of him. The reflection in the mirror. He was not in the right place to date, he told himself.

Pete encouraged him to ask her out.

"She's just a friend," he kept saying.

"Man, she likes you. She is gorgeous," Pete would say.

The *inner* felt Sadia was just a friend as well, but Pete pushed him to pursue her, to ask her out, but Jaxon could be so stubborn sometimes.

Sadia is stunning. Jaxon is an idiot.

With his senses heightened he suddenly felt something different after all these years. Butterflies in his stomach. This pressing urge to be with her, to hold and hug her, to run his hands down her back and squeeze her cheeks. To kiss her. Was this love? Or was it lust? Or a mix of both? Whatever it was, it was exciting!

Seriously, Jaxon you need to rethink this one. we have a lot of talking to do when we reunite. Wait a minute, will we ever rejoin?

That thought terrified him. Then he and Sadia locked eyes. She smiled.

Does she recognize me? Does she know that me and Jaxon are one? It seems like she does.

"Excuse, me! Hello," said Pete interrupting the brief moment between Sadia and the *inner*. "Can I help you?"

He cleared his throat and took a few steps toward
Pete.

Yeah, Pete, it's me.

Pete got out of the chair and walked toward him.

He extended his hand.

"Who are you?" asked Pete.

"Dude, it's me!"

"Hmm. I've never seen you before, wait you're the
guy that was at the accident. Who are you really? And
what are you doing here?" asked Pete.

*"We're actually very close. Closer than what you
think."*

Pete raised his eyebrows. "Interesting. I'm his best
friend, and I've never heard of you."

*"Sorry to disappoint you, but I'm the one he talks to
the most."*

Pete made a *tsk* sound and shook his head. "You
realize that I've never heard of you or seen you. What

kind of scam are you trying to pull here?"

Sadia who was watching the whole interaction in awe got up and stood next to both of them.

"What's going on?" she asked, throwing her hands in the air.

The *inner* was thinking, *Look at that gorgeous silk hair, those eyes, and that perfect figure. Jaxon has been so blind, and that sexy voice is seducing.*

"This man here claims he's Jaxon and he's here to see Jaxon," said Pete.

"Ha! Interesting," said Sadia. "We've never seen you before, and we've known Jaxon all of our lives."

He smiled.

"Where did you meet him?" asked Sadia.

"Listen, I know it's hard for you to understand, but I am Jaxon, we are Jaxon. We know everything about each other."

"Really? We are Jaxon?" said Sadia. "And you know

everything... everything!?"

She is charming, he thought

"Yes, everything."

"Really? Prove it," she demanded.

"My... ah Jaxon's... Our first crush was his sixth grade English teacher Mrs. Fowler."

"What else?"

"My... our... Jaxon's first kiss was when he kissed Mandy Ramirez in my... our backyard."

"Are you Mandy's boyfriend? asked Pete. "Is this a jealousy thing?"

"I told you I know everything. I am Jaxon, we are Jaxon. Do you still want more proof?   Okay, here is one for you. Pete, remember when you had a bike accident when you were 9? You had a cast on your arm for four weeks. I...we... came to your house to sign the cast. Your favorite scribbling was from your crush Kate who wrote. 'You'll always shine. Get better soon.'"

"Did you go to Flower Valley Elementary? Is this how you know Jaxon?" asked Pete. "I don't remember you. Were you one of those nerdy dudes who always sat in the back and never talked?"

"Not really. I was always there though. With Jaxon all the time."

"You're lying," said Sadia. "I've never seen you in my whole life. What do you want?"

He noticed that Sadia was looking at his necklace.

"Okay, here is another one. Sadia loves burgers with two slices of cheese, no pickles and raw onions. Most of her family are vegetarians, though, and think she is, too."

"Dude, who are you?" asked Pete waving his hand.

"Do you believe me now? We... are Jaxon?"

"No. You are a scammer," said Pete. "What do you want? Money? How much?"

"How did you know this?" said Sadia whose face

was turning red.

"Well, I told you I'm, he's...we're Jaxon. I'm always there with him."

"Get out of here," said Pete.

"And Sadia, how is your grandma doing? I know you're worried about her. Is she still dealing with those... issues?" he said, remembering when Sadia confided in Jaxon about her grandma's health problems.

I'm so worried we are going to lose her to that horrible disease, she told Jaxon in between tears. Jaxon pulled her closer to him as she cried in his arms.

"Who told you this? Jaxon? He promised me he wouldn't tell anyone. My family is very private."

He felt like a complete jerk.

"I blew it. I should not have mentioned this. I should not have betrayed Jaxon, Us like that."

"What is he talking about? What's wrong with Grandma?"

"Pete, not now. I don't what to talk about this now," she said her eyes welling with tears.

"Can I please just talk to him?" he asked.

He touched his necklace. He needed to feel that force of energy again. It grounded him. It calmed him.

"No! I told you to get out of here," said Pete.

"Come on, Pete. I promise I won't tell anyone about your crushes. Especially the one you met at the gym."

He immediately regretted what he said. He should not out Pete in this manner. Sadia knew it, too, but none of his other friends. His crush was a woman much older than him. Almost 15 years older, but he was madly in love, and he didn't care about her age.

"Don't listen to others. Rachel is a great woman. She'll make you happy. Don't ever let her ago," he said, parroting what Jaxon told Pete a few nights before the accident.

"Get out of here, you creep," shouted Pete.

Pete charged toward him, and attempted to shove him.

The *inner* use one hand to effortlessly move Pete out the way. Pete regained his balance quickly. He remained calm.

"Please!" he pleaded. *"It'll be only for a few minutes. I came a long way to see him, me, us. Trust me. Getting here was not easy."*

"Just let him see him," said Sadia who shifted her eyes toward Jaxon who was still sound asleep.

"Two minutes, man," said Pete. "Two minutes. If you stay longer, I'll drag you out of this room myself."

"Deal," said the *inner*, then walked toward Jaxon. He was surprised that with all the commotion in the room Jaxon stayed sound asleep. He must be so drugged, he thought. *What are they giving him? Do they even know what they are doing? How good are these doctors?*

Jaxon looked so peaceful, he even had a slight smile

on his face. *Was he dreaming?* The *inner* always enjoyed their dreams, it was like watching a movie to him. Sometimes they were pleasant. He dreamt about his childhood friends. He dreamt about going to the county fair and eating corn dogs. He dreamt about surfing in Hawaii. He dreamt about being in Paris and speaking fluent French.

He also had nightmares. He dreamt about falling, about being in a plane crash, and being chased. He would wake up in the middle of the night and let out a shriek. That was when he would tell Jaxon that everything was fine, that it was just nightmare, that he was right there with him. That he would always protect him no matter what. He missed watching those dreams, and sometimes interacting and being part of his imaginary world, the good, the bad and the ugly.

He examined Jaxon's face. He looked at every detail, still amazed that he was just seeing it in real life for the first time. His pointy nose, his broad jaw, the pimples on his forehead. Even will all of the bruises that covered his face, he was still strong and resilient. *He's a fighter*.

The *inner* just fell into his thought about the accident. He could still hear the screeching of the truck's brakes, Jaxon's thoughts of wanting to get out of the way, and his thoughts of wanting to prevent Jaxon from being hurt. He could still feel the mild pain of the impact on his shoulder. The feel of the front grill. Before they separated he could still remember Jaxon's fear. He remembered everything. The headlights, Jaxon's blood, lots and lots of blood. Then talking to Pete and Sadia, then blackness, the absolute darkness right before he passed out.

The more he replayed the accident in his head the more his emotions were boiling out of control. He kept staring at Jaxon's face. He wanted to tell him that everything would be fine. That he had survived. That they will get through this together. He wanted to be united again, to be whole. He wanted things to go back to how they were before.

While lost in thought, he heard footsteps. He turned around and saw his, Jaxon's parents, Julius and Jenna, entering the room.

He felt the chaos in his mind calm. Here they were. His parents in the flesh. Here he was, in front of them, looking them in the eyes. He wanted to wrap his arms around them. Finally.

"Hello there," said Jenna, as she scanned the room.

That voice. His mom's voice. He knew it so well. She looked even more stunning then he expected her to. She was tall, skinny, with long, silky black hair. She had blue eyes. She was wearing a long green dress. Elegant. She had a golden necklace dangling from her neck. He remembered how much they loved to get hugs from mom.

Jenna's eyes fell on him, and they both stared at each other for what seemed like forever. She walked toward him as her husband Julius trailed behind her.

"Hello," she said almost whispering.

He could see the red circles around her eyes. *Was she crying for me? us? I so want to give her a hug. This might be my only chance.*

"Do I know you from somewhere? You look familiar," she said looking at him intently.

"You do. You know me very well," he smiled, resisting the urge to run to her to hug her.

He could see she was staring at his eight-point star necklace, and the oval-shaped birthmark on his neck. She seemed to be in a trance, transfixed by the *inner's* presence.

"That's a beautiful necklace," Jenna said taking a few steps towards him. She put her hand on his necklace. "I thought it was one of a kind." She caressed it with her thumb and index finger, and then lifted her head and looked at him in the eyes.

The *inner* thought of how much they loved his mom, and how much he worried about her.   How much sadness she had endured especially after losing a year of memories, waking up to a husband and baby, then all of the therapy. In spite of her struggles, she wanted to live. She loved life.

"How do you know my son?" Jaxon's dad, Julius, asked. "I've never seen you before."

"It's a bit complicated," he said, then switched his attention back to Jenna.

"Did you have anything to do with what happened to him?" said Julius, his voice increasing in intensity.

"No, dad, I didn't. I'm the one who saved him."

"Dad? Why are you calling me dad? Young man, what's wrong with you?"

The *inner* took a step toward him. *Dad, you don't*

recognize me? I'm, we're your son."

"What, that's crazy! Did you do this to him? Answer me! Did you do this to him?"

"No, dad, I'm, we're your son. Just look at me. Look me in the eyes," he said pointing his index fingers toward his eyes. *"Look again, please! It's me. Your own flesh and blood."*

"Stop it," shouted Julius, his strong voice reverberating across the room. "I have only one son, and he's definitely not you. My son is right there, in this hospital bed, and he almost died. A miracle saved him. If you had anything to do with this, I swear I'll kill you myself."

Sadia, who looked stunned, grabbed Pete's arm. "What's going on? I'm scared. This is not normal. Who is this guy?"

"I have no clue, but something is not right." said Pete.

The *inner* could still feel Jenna's gaze on him. She was still staring at his necklace and his birthmark. He switched his attention back to her and then their eyes met again. Time froze as they both kept staring at each other.

"I only have one son," said Jenna whispering, as if she was talking to herself.

"Do you really?" he whispered back.

Jenna got silent.

"Just keep looking at me."

"I love your necklace," she said. She was in a trance.

"Thank you," he replied. He felt her warmth. She smelled of lavender. She smelled of home.

"Where did you get it from?" she asked then went back to caressing the necklace as if she was waiting for a genie to emerge from it.

My mother. She gave it to me when I was born. I have never taken it off.

"Honey," said Jenna looking at her husband. "I think

he's ... he's… our son." She looked dazed.

"What are you talking about?" said Julius shaking his head.

"Just look at him. Look at his eyes. He *is* Jaxon. Our Jaxon. I can't explain it, but I know it in my heart. He's ours."

"What did you do to my wife?" said Julius who was almost hyperventilating by that point. "Are you doing some crazy hypnosis stuff? You some sort of a con artist? Who sent you here?"

"Stop it, Julius. Just stop it. I'm fine. He didn't do anything. He's our son. Our flesh and blood."

"Honey, I think you need some rest. You're exhausted." Julius grabbed his wife's hand. "All that sleep deprivation is messing with your head. Let's go to the cafeteria. You need to eat something."

The *inner* could see how agitated Julius was getting, and it worried him. Julius already had heart issues, and their conversation was not headed in the right direction. He didn't expect it to go sour. Not like that. What was he thinking? That they would just accept him with open arms? He had to calm him down.

"Dad! Remember when we lived on Maple Avenue, and we used to take walks every evening," he said then paused to watch Julius's reaction whose face started to turn red.

Remember when we used to sit on the hill at the end of the street and look at the mountains on the horizon?"

Julius raised his eyebrows. "What are you talking about? Is this some sort of voodoo magic?"

"Dad, please stop lying to yourself. Remember when you told me you regretted not going to college, and that you really wanted me to get the best education?"

"Quit it. Just quit."

"Remember our favorite ice-cream shop on Ott street. I always get two chocolate scoops, and you get

the banana split.”

“Who told you all of this?” asked Julius. “Have you been spying on us?”

“Remember when I fell off a cliff in the woods near our house and you carried me all the way to the house? Remember when you teared up that night when you put me to bed saying that I was the best thing that ever happened to you?”

“How do you know all of this? You’re like a professional scammer, aren’t you?” said Julius.

“And you have a birthmark on your lower back. Remember you used to call it the Texas birthmark, because it’s shaped liked the state?”

“Stop,” said Julius, a vain bulging in his forehead. He put his foot forward ready to charge at him. Ready to rip him apart. Tear him to pieces and throw him to the lions.

“And your favorite drink is gin and tonic, Remember

when you let me take a few sips when I was like 13 years old. You told me that I should not let mom know. I think I finished the whole thing that day."

"I want you out of this room now. Now!" shouted Julius.

"Remember when you told me about your dad, and how you found out he was cheating on your mother, and you promised yourself you would never ever do this to your future wife."

"Shut up."

"And remember Jack our next-door neighbor. Remember when you helped him out. You loaned him money so that he could pay his mortgage after he lost his job. You didn't even tell mom about it, but you told me."

"Shut up!" shouted Julius. "Shut up now. I don't want to hear another word from you. Get out of this room now! I don't want to see your face ever again."

"Julius, stop it," said Jenna. "Look at him. Somehow

he is our son.”

“Jenna, stop this nonsense. You’re just tired and in shock. Let me deal with this imposter.”

“Hey,” said Jaxon as he slowly awakened. He looked around the room observing who was there.

“Honey, you’re awake,” said Jenna, then rushed to his side. “You’re feeling better? Glad you got some rest.”

“Hey, I recognize that voice.”

Julius and Jenna switched their attention back to the *inner*. They immediately noticed that Jaxon no longer had his birthmark on his neck. His eight-point star necklace was around this other guy’s neck.

“Jaxon! Your eyes,” shouted Sadia. “Oh my God. Your eyes changed color.”

“Jaxon, honey,” said Jenna. “Your eyes!”

“What’s going on?” said Julius looking at the *inner*.

“What in God’s name is going on? I’m going to call

security."

"Dad, please stop! I recognize that voice, too," said Jaxon whose eyes were somehow blue, and everyone noticed. He put his hand on his face. "Ouch, it hurts when I talk."

"Honey, just rest," said Jenna. "The medicines are causing havoc on you, I'm sure."

"Am I dreaming?" asked Jaxon addressing his mom. "I'm hearing voices. Imagining things. Crazy things." He let out a big sigh. "And what's wrong with my eyes?" he asked.

"Nothing honey, nothing. Don't worry about. I'm sure it's just a side effect from the all the medicine they are giving you."

"I'm losing my mind," Jaxon said as he lifted himself and sat up in the bed. Jenna helped him position himself.

"You need to take it easy, sweetheart," she said, then

tucked a strand of his hair behind his ear. "I'll ask the doctor about your eyes. I'm sure it's something temporary."

"Mom, I'm a mess."

"I love you, baby. Everything will be okay. You're just tired and in so much pain. We're just so grateful that you're live. We almost lost you," she said then started crying.

"Don't cry, mom, please don't," he said between sobs. He rubbed his eyes and focused his attention on the *inner*. He closed his eyes and then opened them again. He rubbed his eyes again.

"You're the voice in my head," said Jaxon looking at him in awe, hardly believing that he was seeing him in person. Flesh and bones. "You are that person that I see every time I look in the mirror?"

"*I am,*" he said, smiling.

"What person? Have you been breaking into our

house? Jaxon, explain this. What the heck is going on?" said Julius.

"You're me. I know you are me. The *inner* me. I so wanted to meet you. I waited for this moment all my life. Is this real? Please tell me I'm not dreaming," said Jaxon.

"No. You're not dreaming. I'm right here in front of you."

Jaxon wiped off his tears with the back of his hand and stared at him. "Wow, you look exactly how I saw you in the mirror. I thought my mind was playing tricks on me every time I looked in the mirror. You are here. The same person I've been seeing all my life, but why are you here? You're not supposed to be out here. What's going on? Help me understand. I'm losing my mind."

The *inner* sighed. *"I don't know what really happened. I'm still trying to figure it out."*

"But how can it be? It doesn't make any sense."

"I don't know. We just have to accept it for now."

"So are you telling me that you're the one who influenced me to do all this crazy stuff?" asked Jaxon smiling.

He laughed. *"Yeah, that was me."*

"That was you? I can't believe I listened to you all these years. "

Jenna was listening to their conversation smiling while Julius had his arms crossed and looked like he was about to explode. Pete and Sadia were both shaking their heads in disbelief.

"And what's with the mayonnaise on asparagus? That's just gross. Can't believe you made me eat that nastiness."

"It's delicious!"

"No! Everyone thinks I'm disgusting. You just keep embarrassing me."

Jaxon's parents' eyes switched between Jaxon and the *inner* like a ping pong ball.

"How did we separate?" asked Jaxon.

"I don't know. I had no control over what happened, but I have a theory. You know right before the accident happened, I think for the first time in our life we wanted different things. Remember you wanted to stay and gamble, I wanted to leave, you wanted to bar hop I wanted to go home, you wanted to run away from the truck, and I wanted to stop it. We made 2 completely different decisions. I Believe our wills clashed and we separated. I think that's what happened."

"Ha! That makes sense. That makes total sense," said Jaxon who then lowered his head and closed his eyes as if he was in deep thought. He opened his eyes and looked at the *inner*. "I just feel so, so weak."

"You do," he said.

"It's not just from the accident. It's this hollowness,

this emptiness. It's so hard to describe. I feel like a shell of my former self." He sighed. "I don't know, man. I just feel less without you." He shook his head.

"You know what's weird?"

"What?" asked Jaxon.

"Well. Hard to explain it, but I feel totally the opposite from you."

"How so?"

"I feel much stronger, powerful, my senses are so heightened now, but I am a little exhausted." He looked down at his hands and clenched his fists. *"I'm feeling something strange now. Right here."* He placed his hand on his necklace and started fiddling with it.

"What is it? Are you okay?"

"Can you guys cut the melodrama. This is crazy," shouted Julius.

"Dad, please give us a minute."

"I'm just feeling this massive force. It's pulling me.

It's pulling me toward you. I can't stop it. I can't resist it."

He extended his arms as if he was trying to keep himself balanced.

Jaxon, who was wearing his hospital gown, got out of the bed without hesitation, dragging the IV pole behind him, and stood next to the *inner*. It seemed he immediately understood what was going on as if that strong force was pulling him, too, dragging him towards the *inner*.

Jaxon' parents, Pete, and Sadia watched as Jaxon and the *inner* stood next to each other, their hips touching. To their utter shock, Jaxon and the *inner's* bodies slowly began to merge, to mesh together. They all watched in disbelief.

Jenna let out a scream.

"Oh My God," shouted Sadia. "What's going on? Someone tell me what's going on!"

A blinding bright beam of flight flashed out of nowhere illuminating the whole room.

Pete, Sadia, and Jaxon's parents covered their eyes with their hands. When they opened them, they couldn't believe what they were seeing right in front of them. While the *inner* was merging with Jaxon's, it appeared as if they were also transforming, his eight-point necklace reappeared, and his birthmark was resurrected on Jaxon's neck.

Eventually, the *inner* completely merged within Jaxon, and Jaxon was left standing barefoot in his nightgown. He closed his eyes and took a deep breath. He exhaled. His eyes were brown again.

"I feel so much better," said Jaxon. "So much better. I feel healed. Completely healed. He took all my pain away," he said as his bruises started to disappear from his face in front of everyone's eyes. He touched his face.

"I feel fresh. Like I've been reborn," he said.

Both Sadia and Pete had tears streaming down their cheeks. Everyone in the room felt the intensity of the emotions.

"That was overwhelming," said Jaxon looking at Jenna. "Mom, I'm ready to go home."

"Yeah, sweetheart we'll take you home," said Jenna.

Pete and Sadia were frozen in place. They kept looking at each other in disbelief.

"What did we just see?" asked Sadia.

"I have no clue. No clue. This was not natural. This was something beyond all of us," said Pete whose face had turned completely white, deprived of all color.

"I'm scared. I'm scared for Jaxon, for all of us. What did he get himself into?"

Pete put his arms around Sadia giving her a side hug. "I don't think he got himself into anything."

"What do you mean?" asked Sadia who was shivering with tears streaming down her face.

"I think he has always been like this."

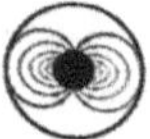

A new force is building. Not here before me,

though I sense it as plain as the surface of my skin.

Somewhere beyond the desert sands and ocean waves, a

great power awakens. It reverberates through the ground

and comes wafting in the air—a rush more fierce than

the great river and a brilliance more stunning than gold.

Though it journeys from a distance to greet me, this new

power comes wielding capacities that this world could

never comprehend.

While I may shift the planet at my will, I sense that this

power could expand or collapse it, should it choose. It

could warp the planet's very magnetism! Though I know of

no power that could possibly claim such might, I fear it easily eclipses my own. Were it to decide, I sense that this power could come to alter the very celestial order binding the universe.

What is this flash that comes cresting the dunes? Not the sky's fiery eye, bringer of light and life, rather a flash of darkness across its path?

An ominous black flame flickers out the rising sun's brightness. Small though it may be, this empty glimmer holds me captive in its dance. Its movements echo into a force field of music, ensnaring me with its song. Even the planet's polar magnetism has shifted to match its choreography.

Without its usual day breaking levity, the great sky star has stopped cold in its shallow heights. Watching this peculiar black flame consume its nascent morning light, the sun staggers, much as I have, at the sight. With bated breath, both the sun and I wait for its bidding before we make our next move.

Though, at present, it is but the spark of a flint, it weighs upon me. Heavier than the very metal of heaven—this weight carries with it the power to absorb all other particles, even more, I sense, than this world has to offer.

What dark raven dare flap so close to the mighty solar path lest its feathered wings, too, be made of fire, or worse? The very wind that bears its flight brings with it ominous news. It whispers of a great inferno to come—a power that could dissolve the sun in its orbit, should it choose.

I sense this arrival under my skin, within my very molecules. Beyond the dry horizon, somewhere across the great skydome, it already seeps into all it touches.

The winged feline kings that guard the ancients would crumble at its feet. No jeweled scarab talisman might resist its coming, nor the power that it will grow to wield. Now, as it conquers the day and its brilliance, the might of this dark magnet draws me into its incipient force.

Already, its power has me under its command.

With this dawn comes a great crack of silence—the might of this budding force hammering upon the ancient laws, long etched in stone. I sense this dark fire operates within a whole new realm of power, all of which falls under its control.

I fear even the celestial order that binds the universe will have to choose: comply with the will of this new rising power or be consumed by its might.

Chapter 6

Love "Absorbed"

July 24,2018br

8:00AM

Jaxon sat by the window next to Sadia in the backseat of his parents' 4 door SUV. The three of them, Jaxon, Pete, and Sadia were crammed in the back as Julius offered to give everyone a ride back home.

"No one is taking a taxi today," commanded Julius. "Everyone is coming with me," he said, his eyebrows crossed, face flushed, and voice hoarse.

No one argued. They all dragged themselves silently to the car and climbed in. Pete and Sadia were winded, barely communicating, barley moving, as if they had just emerged from a war zone in which no one won.

As they all got settled in the backseat, Jaxon felt his thigh rubbing against Sadia's. He felt the urge to put his hand on hers but stopped himself at the last minute. Instead, he placed his hand on his pair of blue jeans. He rubbed his hands back and forth thinking.

We need to hold her, comfort her, let her know that everything is ok

She looked up at him and smiled.

Is she feeling what we're feeling? Does she feel the chemistry between us? Or is she creeped out by what she saw?

"Are you okay?" she asked.

"Much better. Thank you for being there for me."

"Always," she said still smiling, her eyes twinkling

as if she was on the verge of tears.

They locked eyes, and he could see her face was getting flushed. She laughed nervously, lowered her head, and looked at the phone in her hand.

He took this as a sign as he gathered enough courage to hold her hand.

Before he could she reached over and squeezed his hand.

He smiled as he noticed she still cared. He switched his attention to his parents.

As Julius was driving, Jenna was in the driver seat looking out the window at the passing streets, her head resting on the glass, and her face pale. She looked as if she was going to pass out at any moment. The radio was off, and all that could be heard was the humming of the car as it sped along the quiet streets. The silence was deafening as everyone seemed to be in shock or in a trance, or just lost in thoughts.

Jaxon felt guilty. How would they ever get over what they had just seen at the hospital?

Will they ever talk to me again, or will they just be too scared to come near me? he wondered.

Jaxon looked straight and noticed that his dad was gripping the steering wheel so hard he could see veins bulging in his hands.

Not good. Not good at all.

Jaxon was mostly concerned about his dad. He would never forgive himself if something happened to him.

Jaxon leaned his head back and thought of what had happened since the accident. What transpired was hard to comprehend, especially for his dad who was a man of science. It defied any and all logic to him.

He knew his dad felt powerless, and feeling powerless never sat well with him for he saw himself as the protector of his family. Jaxon was well aware that his dad would be disappointed in himself for failing to control the situation, but really, how could he control the supernatural?

Jenna felt his gaze on him, so she looked up and smiled. Jaxon suddenly noticed the wrinkles under her eyes. When did that happen? Was he so consumed with his life that he didn't notice that his mom was aging, that she was not immortal?

He sighed then looked back at Sadia from the corner of his eye. She was staring at her phone, head down, legs bouncing up and down.

Aw Sadia. She must be in extreme shock.

Pete was already asleep, his head slumped forward, drool coming out of his mouth. Jaxon could hear his deep breathing, and every once in a while he would let out a snore. Pete was one of the lucky ones. He always handled stress with sleep.

Jaxon fidgeted in the leather seat, then looked

outside the window, as they were driving through small suburban streets covered with trees and cookie cutter houses. Very few people were out. It was a little after 8:00 a.m. Besides a few dog walkers, and a few smokers, the suburb dwellers were still sleeping in, and cuddled with their loved ones. Everyone was busy with their own little life, thought Jaxon. No one was aware that there was more to life than what they had. They were oblivious to the big picture.

What a shame, he thought.

Jaxon exhaled, and thought about his life. He thought about that short video that played in front of him right as he was hit by the truck. Right before he thought that his life was over, cut short. Right before he felt it was his time to cross to the other side. He was not sure how long that video was, but it seemed fast, one image after the other, flashing in front of his eyes.

He saw himself as a child building a sandcastle on

the beach along with his older cousins. He saw himself

going down the slide in his neighborhood playground,

his arms up in the air. Then his dad pushing him in a

swing while he sang *Ring around the Rosie*. Seeing

himself in a classroom on the first day of Kindergarten.

His eyes were teary as he missed his mom. Being with

his dad on a baseball field. He was gripping a bat while

his dad was getting ready to throw a pitch.

Reliving moments of fishing with his dad.

"Look dad I caught a big one!"

"Great job buddy! I guess your mom doesn't have to

worry about dinner tonight."

Running after an ice cream truck.

"Stop! Stop! I want an ice cream sandwich!"

Seeing his parents and friends singing Happy

Birthday to him, him flashing the number eight with his

fingers. Riding his bike in the woods, the wind going

through his hair. Playing soccer with his mom.

"You are good at this, buddy! We need to put you in

a league."

He saw himself looking outside an airplane window

as they were headed to Florida to see his grandparents,

and playing video games in the backseat of a car,

headphones on, while he was munching on Doritos.

Then he saw a big bright light and then he saw her.

Sadia.

On the first day of Kindergarten, as they both sat

around a small table. She had two braids and a pink hair

band. She was looking around at everyone in the

classroom with her wide brown eyes.

Jaxon saw himself offering her his bag of goldfish

crackers.

He saw her laughing at his jokes as the three of them,

Pete, Jaxon, and Sadia sat around a wooden round table

at Carlo's, their neighborhood pizza place.

Remembering her looking at him with a twinkle in

her eyes.

Sadia.

Her in their neighborhood's pool wearing a pink bikini and reading a book as she sat cross-legged in the grass. He saw himself sitting next to her, as he did his best not to look at her breasts and asked her about the book she was reading.

He saw her sitting on the bleachers in high school cheering for him as their school's football team played against the "rich kids" school team.

He saw her crying after finding out about her grandmother's health issues. He wrap his arms around her, telling her that everything would be okay.

Sadia!

He saw her teaching him how to sway to Shakira's *Ojos Asi* as they were both on the dance floor at one of their high school house parties. She had her hands on his hips and was moving them sideways as he laughed and told her that he was not born to be a dancer.

He saw her in his car as he dropped her off one night after they went bowling with their classmates. He saw the twinkle in her eyes, her smile. He felt the electricity. She wanted him that night, but he didn't do anything. He just told her goodnight and gave her a kiss on the check.

Sadia!

Beautiful. Sweet. Charming. Smart. Funny. Sexy. Compassionate. Ambitious. Empathetic. How foolish was he not to make her his?

He turned his head and looked at Sadia again. Really looked at her.

She felt his gaze and lifted her head from her phone. She smiled. She looked tired, black circles under her eyes, and her black wavy hair was messy, but was still gorgeous.

I'm a fool. How didn't I see this? How did I not pay her any attention?

Jenna turned around and looked at him.

"Are you okay, hon?"

"Yeah, yeah. I'm fine. Back to my old self," he smiled. He could see tears welling up in her eyelids.

"I feel better than before," he said. "Are *you* okay?"

"Yeah, hon. Just tired. I need a good night's sleep."

When they stopped by Pete's house, Jaxon hit him on his shoulder.

"Pete, you're home."

Pete opened his eyes and looked around. He looked at Jaxon.

"Are you okay, man? Did I dream what happened at the hospital?"

"It happened," said Jaxon.

"Unbelievable," said Pete shaking his head. "Do you need anything?"

"I'm fine. Thank you for being there for me."

"Of course."

He tapped him on the shoulder.

"Just take care, man," he said, and then got out of the car and walked to his house, a small green tri-level at the end of a cul-de-sac.

When they arrived at Sadia's apartment building, she squeezed Jaxon's hand then got out.

Jaxon felt a rush of feelings run through him.

* * *

When they got home, Jaxon went straight to his room. He plopped on the bed and let out a big sigh. The duvet cover was soft and smelled of fresh laundry. The smell of home.

He looked around at the bookshelf in front of him. Fantasy books, Boy Scouts medals, and baseball trophies lined the wooden shelves.

I have a good life. My parents did everything in their

might to make me happy.

He closed his eyes to get some rest as his thought replayed the short movie in his mind. The one that flashed in front of him as he was about to lose his life.

"Sadia". He said as he snapped out of his dream.

It has always been her.

That was the only thing that he could think of.

He pulled his phone from his pocket, and realized he slept most of the day away. There were a number of missed messages. Friends checking on him. Cousins and family too. He pressed select all and deleted all of them. He needed to focus. He noticed a few drops of blood on the back of his phone. His blood. The image of the accident flashed in front of him and he felt his breath stop for a second, then he sent a text message to Sadia.

How are you? I know you've seen a lot today. I need to explain things.

Can I come over?

He heard a knock on the door. His mom peeked her head around the door.

"Honey, come down to eat something. We have some leftover roast."

Jaxon suddenly realized that he was famished.

"Thanks, mom. I'll come down soon."

"Don't take too long. Your dad is already waiting, and he's not in a great mood."

At the kitchen table, they all ate in silence. The grandfather clock mounted on the wall across from the kitchen chimed loudly breaking the silence.

"Are you okay?" his dad asked.

Jaxon nodded, staring at the food on his plate

All he could think of was Sadia. Her smile, her hair, her lean body. Her smell. The way she looked at him in her car. Her voluptuous long legs. Her perfect breasts. Her sexy seductive voice.

He checked his phone.

No response.

He tapped his fingers on the table while chewing slowly on a piece of roast. He watched his mom pass a bowl of potato salad to his dad.

They both looked at him silently.

"Your eyes, they're just different," said Jenna.

"They'll be fine in a few days," said Julius. "I'm sure it's a reaction to the medication. Don't worry."

"Mom, dad, I know you're in shock," said Jaxon. "I really can't explain what happened. I just, knew I was different since I was really young."

Jenna put down her cutlery on the table. "I know, honey," she said as tears started streaming down her face. "I know you're different. I'm your mother. I sense these things."

"Mom, you know the guy who was in the hospital, who is now, you know, inside of me?"

"How can I ever forget?" she asked then lifted her

glass of wine with her shaky hand and took a sip.

"I hear his voice in my head all the time. I've been seeing his reflection in the mirror since I was a baby. I never told you this. I kept these things to myself. I was worried you'd think I'm messed up in the head."

"There's nothing wrong with you!" his dad blurted out and then banged the table with his fist.

"That guy was doing some magic tricks on all of us. I don't want to see his face ever again. If I do, I'm going to-"

"No, Dad. He was not doing any magic. He's me," Jaxon said pointing at himself with his index finger.

"Stop with this talk. Stop it," Julius shouted. "You're my son! I watched you come to life. I saw you take your first step. I taught you how to ride a bike, how to drive a car. Stop this talk about that guy being you."

"Honey, maybe we need to listen to Jaxon to understand more," Jenna said as she placed her hand on his.

"There's nothing to understand. I don't want to hear about that con artist anymore. Do you all hear me? I don't want anyone to mention what happened at the hospital ever again. I want everyone to pretend it never happened." Julius said as his face was getting redder by the minute.

Jaxon got worried that his dad might choke on the piece of roast he had in his mouth.

"My job is to protect you. That's why I live on this earth. This charlatan is not going to rip our family apart. Does everyone hear me?"

Jenna got quiet, and then squeezed his hand. "Babe, everything is fine. Our son is here with us. He's healthy. We're all one family together. We're all safe, and we all love you."

Jaxon took a sip from his water. He didn't have any more words to add. He felt he was suffocating.

"Excuse me," he announced. "And, by the way, my eyes will stay brown. They are never going back to blue."

He went back to his room and checked his phone. Still no response. He sent another message.

Is it okay if I come over?

I really need to explain things.

Fifteen minutes passed and still no response.

What are we waiting for?

Jaxon put on his running shoes and as he was getting ready to leave the house, his hand on the door handle, he heard his mom's voice behind him.

"Where are you going, honey? Are you okay?"

"Just going out for a walk. I need to blow off steam."

She put both of her hands on his shoulder. "You just got home from the hospital."

"Mom, I'm fine, really. Completely fine. I need to get some air."

She sighed and gave him a hug. "I love you, Jaxon. Be safe out there."

"I will. How is dad? I'm a little worried about him."

"He'll be better. He just went to sleep. It's really hard for him to wrap his head around what just happened. He has never been a believer in anything he can't explain."

"I know. I just feel like it's all my fault."

"Don't think that, you are not to blame. You are just being you."

He gave her a kiss on the cheek, and then left the house.

He stood on the sidewalk for a second to collect his thoughts, as he enjoyed the cool breeze. He looked up at the sky, there were no stars in sight. He let out a big sigh, and then started walking.

He put Sadia's address in his GPS, a five mile walk. That should give me some time to clear my head, he told himself. He thought about his life. His parents, and most importantly her. Sadia. The one and only.

As his emotions and excitement start to build uncontrollably, he started to feel this massive force of energy coursing through his veins. He felt this energy pulsing non-stop as goosebumps sprang up all over his body. The buildup was so rapid and intense that he had to release this energy somehow.

I have never felt this strong, this powerful, we can do anything.

He took a deep breath and inhaled the cool breeze. He looked at his hands, then he curled his fingers into a fist. He felt this pressing need release it, to release that power that was growing inside of him, suffocating him.

He started breathing heavily, almost panting, and then felt a bit lightheaded from the enormous amount of energy that he was feeling. He kept on walking. The urge to punch something got stronger and stronger by the minute. He stopped by the first tree he saw and punched its trunk with all his force. His hand went through the maple tree making a deep hole as if he had punched a plywood wall.

"Dude, what was that, for?" shouted a young man who was walking across the street.

Jaxon pulled his hand out of the tree and looked at the guy.

"Just blowing off some steam, man."

"That's one hell of a punch," said another man who was out jogging.

"I have a lot of energy today." Said Jaxon

"I can see that. Take it easy, man!"

"I'll do my best," said Jaxon, who waved goodbye and then kept on walking.

He took a closer look at his hand. It was unscathed. No scratches, no blisters, no blood, no bruises. Nothing, as if he had run his hand in clay instead of a tree trunk.

What are we now? We are more powerful than we have ever been. More powerful than anyone I know.

His energy kept building. Even after making a hole in a tree trunk, he was filled with energy.

He had to see Sadia.

"That's the only thing that is going to calm me," he thought.

He kept walking, feeling like he was about to explode. The more he thought of her the more his energy grew. The amount of energy running through him was so immense that he had to stop a couple of times to release it. On a tree trunk, a brick wall, a car, a dumpster, a street sign, just about anything in his path.

"Dude, what are you doing? I'm calling the police!" yelled a man who was standing by the corner of the street smoking a cigarette.

Jaxon ignored him, and just kept on walking.

He kept walking, breathing intensely. He heard

someone shout, "Rex, stop, stop now! Rex!"

He looked up and saw a dog running toward him on the sidewalk, his long leash trailing behind. His frantic owner sprinting behind trying to catch up with him.

"Rex, Rex, stop!"

The dog ran toward Jaxon. It seemed enraged, ready to attack.

Jaxon looked at the dog and wished the dog would just leave him alone. His mind imagined the dog being tied up to the fence, and just like that the dog was completely wrapped up in his own leash, tied to the fence. The owner caught up with it and was completely baffled by what he saw.

"What just happened?" the dog owner said looking at his dog. "Rex are you okay?"

The dog whimpered as he tried to untie it.

"Did you do this?" asked the perplexed dog owner.

Jaxon shrugged and walked away with his hands in

the pockets.

We are growing stronger, Can you feel it, too?

"Yes," Jaxon responded

"We can control things with just a thought."

"If this is true, we are unbelievable, maybe even invincible."

Jaxon rubbed his face with his hands. He was confused, puzzled by what was happening to him. He let out a big sigh and kept walking. He passed a Ford Mustang parked in the driveway of a McMansion.

I hate Mustangs.

And I hate McMansions.

Should we do something about this monstrosity?

With his mind, he made a dogwood tree planted in the front yard fall right on top of the car. *Crank!* A loud deafening noise reverberated across the neighborhood. The car alarm went off.

Jaxon's heart skipped a beat. He really didn't expect

that to happen so easily. He had so much power. He looked at the car. Its roof got split in half as one of the tree branches went through it and ripped the driver seat.

He watched as the owner of the house, a man with white hair, pot belly, and glasses came out of his house wearing flannel pajamas.

"My car!! what just happened?" Jaxon heard him say as he looked at the car. He watched him bang on his head with both of his hands, run inside his house and come back out with a cellphone and car keys.

He walked around the car, disarmed the alarm, then inspected the roof. He took a step back and dialed his phone.

"I would like to report an emergency," the McMansion owner said, the cellphone glued to his ear.

Jaxon watched as perplexed neighbors rushed out of their houses to look at the destruction that had just happened in their neighborhood.

I feel much better now.

Jaxon continued walking. Three miles left to Sadia's house. They flew by quickly as he spent most of his time testing his newfound power. With his mind doing the impossible. He never felt more powerful.

***

July 24,2018br

7:01PM

When he found himself right in front of Sadia's apartment building, he felt energized. He wasn't even winded. He felt he had enough energy to compete in a marathon or triathlon. He felt on top of the world.

He looked at the apartment complex where Sadia lived. It was tucked away in a woodsy area, where wildlife was abundant. A couple of deer were up on the hill, which surrounded the complex. They were scavenging for food. Although it was dark, it was easy for him to see them. Even his eyesight seemed to have improved after the *inner* merged.

He was not surprised that Sadia chose this place. She had always valued her privacy.

He walked to the building's entrance and looked at the cars parked in front. Her Toyota was parked at its usual place. He walked up the stairs to the first floor where her apartment was. He looked at the white wooden door, which was bare expect for a peephole. He took a deep breath.

He pondered for a second, then rang the bell. He could feel the nervous energy building and beating of his heart in his throat. Was this excitement or was it fear? Either way, he was ready to face it.

Jaxon had no patience left. He had to see her! *Right now*! He thought about blowing the door off the henges, and just like that he heard a loud sound and the door blew off the hinges. Pieces of wood chips flew in the air. As he was dusting himself off, he heard a commotion and saw Sadia running toward the door.

His heart was thumping so loudly at just the sight of her.

There she is with all her glory. the love of my life.

She was still dressed in the same clothes she had on at the hospital. Skinny dark blue jeans and a red long-sleeved shirt. Her hair was disheveled as if she just had woken up from a nap. She had black socks on and no shoes.

"Oh my God," said Sadia as she saw the door. She looked up. "Jaxon?" she said raising her eyebrows.

He took two steps inside.

Jaxon looked around her apartment. Nothing had changed since he was there the last time when Sadia had him and some friends over for game night. The worn-out brown leather sofa was still there in the middle of the main room. The TV was mounted on the table. The plants were still in the same place on a small table next to the sofa. The white carpet was still there, although it looked a bit more stained than the last time.

Jaxon was disappointed. He was not sure why.

We can change this. we can do anything!

Jaxon thought about a romantic setting, and just like that everything he wanted just appeared. The brown sofa was replaced by a white love seat. On the seat were rose petals formed in a heart shape.

The lights were dim. The white carpet disappeared into thin air and was replaced by dark hardwood floors. Light lavender scented candles appeared on every surface in the room, and more rose petals emerged on the floor.

"Tear Drop" by Massive Attack started playing from brand new speakers, which appeared next to the TV.

Sadia looked around.

"What's going on?"

"I can't stop thinking about you," he said tilting his head.

"Did you do this? How? Are you some sort of a superhero?" she asked scanning her surroundings, her jaw wide open.

He took her hand and kissed it. She smelled of lavender.

"I've been thinking about you nonstop since I got back from the hospital."

Her skin was soft, and her hand fit perfectly inside his.

"Same here," whispered Sadia looking him in the eyes. "What happened out there at the hospital?" She sighed. "I really can't wrap my head around it."

"Don't think much about it, Sadia. I'm here to see you. I'm here for you. That's what matters now. Nothing else."

They locked eyes, then he gave her a long kiss. She tasted of sugar and honey, of chocolate and agave, of syrup and stevia, of nectar, of all the sweetness in the world rolled into one. He wanted to keep kissing her until there was no tomorrow.

"We are meant to be together, Sadia. I'm sure of it now."

Sadia responded by kissing him back. Their kiss lingered as they both closed their eyes.

When Jaxon opened his eyes, he noticed that both of their clothes were piled in a heap on the floor. He looked at Sadia. She was wearing red lingerie. She was stunning. He felt he was on fire. He had to touch her to quell the flames inside him.

Sadia looked down at her lingerie and ran her fingers through the fabric.

"This is so pretty," she said then looked up at him.

He was wearing black silk underwear. He wrapped his arms around her. He felt a force of euphoria running through his veins.

This feels right. So right.

He looked at Sadia and saw the desire in her eyes. A hunger for him. For his flesh. He put his arms around her waist, then lifted her as he placed her arms around his neck. She was light and he was strong, very strong. He felt he could lift the pyramids of Egypt if he wanted to. He started carrying her to the bedroom, his heart thumping so loudly he thought she might hear it. As he was doing so he felt a lightness in his body and suddenly both of them began floating in the air vertically, up and up almost touching the ceiling.

"I can't believe what's happening. It feels like I died and went to heaven," she said her arms still around his neck.

Then by an unseen force, they got separated and

started floating parallel.

Sadia was smiling through all of it.

Jaxon took a twirl in the air and then wrapped himself around her, pulling her close. With an effortless wave of his free hand, her lingerie and his underwear vanished, while his other arm kept her close to him. He started kissing her passionately.

She tucked her head in the crock of his neck breathing him in.

He ran his hand on her soft skin, on her neck, on her breasts, on her toned belly, and then down in between her legs. She jerked backward as she let out a faint moan.

"Make love to me," she said biting her lip in between her moans that were getting louder by the minute.

He gave her a long kiss, then entered her as they twirled in the air like two mating love birds. He was slow and tender at first, then he pushed harder and faster, then to a slow pace. She moved her head sideways as she took him in, drinking him in, all of him. Her eyes were closed and she was moaning in pleasure.

They seemed oblivious to their location, as their love making took over their consciousness. They kept twirling in the air between red silk sheets, twirling as he was continuously changing from Jaxon to the *inner* to Jaxon back to the *inner*, landing all over the bedroom, on the walls, on the ceiling, on the bed, and back in the air. Up, down, sideways, then up and down again.

Jaxon and the *inner* felt her climaxing multiple times, once, twice, dozens of times. She rolled her eyes, jerked her head back, and curled her cute toes. They both felt her convulsing underneath him. A rush of passion overwhelmed them.

She is mine. "She's mine."

They wanted to memorize every surface of her tender body. Every mole, every scar, every birthmark. The feel of her breasts in their hand, the shape of her nose, her ears, the size of her belly button, the beauty of her sex, the sounds of her pleasure, the way she guided him to her pleasure spots. During their love making, she was both shy and demanding. A mix that excited them, suffocated them with pleasure.

They couldn't get enough of their bodies intertwined, as if they were bound to be one entity together forever. The walls around them started changing colors from white to red to blue, back to red, back to white. The cornucopia of colors reflected on their faces as they couldn't let go of each other. They were unbreakable.

He felt warm. Happy. She felt home.

Hours after hours passed as they floated above the bed. They kept changing positions, Jaxon on top, Sadia on top. The *inner* on top. Doing their best to pleasure each other. Eventually, they all climaxed at the same time, letting out a simultaneous scream of pleasure that rattled the walls.

"Oh, Jaxon."

Her body started to change color slowly. From brown, to light brown, to white, until it became completely transparent. Her eyes were open, and she kept looking at the ceiling as if she was observing a celestial entity.

"I love you. Very much," she said then she completely merged into his body disappearing in thin air. She let out a soft moan as she took her last exit from the world.

Woosh!

Just like that she was gone.

"Sadia," he let out a shout. They wanted her back. They just had her after all this time. We just made love to her.

"Sadia! Don't go! Don't leave me! I need you more now than ever!"

Jaxon's body jerked, then he felt a strong force of energy running all though his veins, his body pulsed.

He stood up and got out of the bed placing his feet on the cold hard wood floor. He was still trying to catch his breath. He looked around the room as if he was hoping to find her nearby. As if she should still be there.

Oh Sadia!

He looked down at this naked body, and felt a force going through him. He lifted his arms up and looked up at the sky.

He suddenly felt a calm. He felt balanced. Mentally at peace. Serene.

I feel good. Balanced.

He heard some commotion outside the bedroom. He got out of the bedroom and walked to the front room, not bothering to put on any clothes.

"What in God's name is going on?" asked a middle-aged man who looked puzzled as if he had seen a dead body.

"Who are you?" asked Jaxon.

"I'm John, the neighbor across the hall, and you?"

"I'm a friend."

"Where is Sadia? And what the hell happened to the door?"

"All is well. Sadia is."

"I don't see her," said John peaking his head inside.

"She's fine, please go home."

"I'm not going home until I see her, and for God's sake put some pants on."

John took a step inside the apartment and scanned the surroundings.

"What happened in here? What happened to her furniture?"

Jaxon clenched his jaw. "Can you please mind your own business, and just go back to your apartment."

"I'm not going anywhere until I see Sadia."

Jaxon curled his fingers into a fist. He was ready to punch him, but he felt so calm and relaxed, so he decided not to. "Man, why are you ruining my good mood like this? I just had the best night of my life."

"I'm sure you did."

"Please leave, everything is fine," said Jaxon.

"I'm not going anywhere until I see Sadia."

Jaxon closed his eyes and with his mind slid a piece of debris under John's foot.

"What the hell?" shouted John as he fell on his back, his glasses flying in the air.

"Ah! My back!" He sat up and picked up his glasses from the floor. He began to make his way toward his apartment yelling.

"I'm calling the police, You're a monster. What did you do to Sadia? Did you rape her? Did you kill her? You won't get away with this!"

Life is balance.

There is no birth without death, no creation without destruction. What is springs from the bones of what was.

This is known.

This is truth.

The spirits of all things resonate in harmony when there is balance. Energy flows like a river, seeking its natural course. As a river feeds the land, nourishing the plants and trees and animals, so, too, energy feeds all living things. This is harmony, conservation of all that is and was and will be. This truth has been passed down from the spirits to their earth children and from them to their children. The birds of the sky know it, the beasts of the earth know it, the creatures of the seas know it. Thus, it has always been.

Until now.

As a pebble disturbs the pond, something new disturbs

the universe. It is not balanced. It is energy, chaotic,

unbounded, troubled.

I have felt it. I have seen the long shadow of its

presence though I cannot yet see its true form. Whether it is

a force for good or for evil cannot be known. By one's

actions a thing, a creature is known. Some take without

thought, others give without sorrow.

It remains to be seen what this will do. I have sensed it

growing but have not been able to know its heart, its true

purpose and intention. I suspect whatever this power is

does not yet know itself. For in knowing itself, it would

create ripples that could be read like the clouds in the sky,

like the tracks of the stag by the river, like the countenance

of one who feels sorrow or joy, guilt or benevolence,

compassion or hatred.

I have lived long and seen much. I have not seen this

before. This eruption of something from what was nothing

is counter to the laws set down long ago. These eyes have not seen this before. These ears have not heard the discordant sounds of the flow of time and space being torn asunder before. These hands have not touched something that has no name or shape or form yet looms so large on the horizon.

Because of this, I do not know by what name I shall yet call it. So, I wait, until it should reveal itself fully and I shall know it. I wait, with the patience that comes from knowing that nothing can long remain hidden. I wait, knowing that intention will soon reveal itself. I wait, and I ponder how this will change the order, in which direction this will push the world out of balance.

Chapter 7

Ascension

July 25,2018br

7:01 AM

With only a thought, Jaxon changed Sadia's room back to how it was before he made his grand entrance. He even made the bed.

"Try to leave the world a little better than you found it," he said out loud, remembering the Boy Scouts' motto of his younger years.

Without lifting a finger, he got himself fully dressed: black jeans, white shirt, blue sneakers. With just a thought he repaired Sadia's apartment door.

He trotted out of the building, his hands in the pockets of his jeans. He felt invigorated. He whistled a tune as he walked away from her apartment building, sniffing the cold early morning air.

"I'm calling the police now," he heard the neighbor, John, shout at the top of his lungs. He dialed his cell phone,

"Hi Officer Sparks. I would like to report some suspicious activity."

Jaxon went back to whistling the tune of "We Are the Champions". He had no care in the world. He just had the best time in his life, and nothing else mattered, not John and his pettiness, not Officer Sparks. Nothing.

"You're despicable. You're not going to get away with what you did to Sadia," he heard John shout as he kept on walking and whistling.

He saw John open his mouth and let out a few more words, but he was no longer listening.

John needs to gets laid.

Jaxon continued walking.

***

The sky had a tint of orange as the sun was rising. He sniffed the crisp air and smiled. The five miles back to his house were uneventful. The streets were filled with the usual suburbs dwellers. The dog walkers, the mothers pushing their babies in strollers, the kids waiting for the school bus, the old couple dragging a shopping cart.

He felt serene, at peace, as if all the energy that he had earlier had been put to good use, flooding him with a massive dose of endorphins.

When he got to his house, he went upstairs to his

room and plopped on the bed, feeling the comforting touch of clean sheets.

He leaned his head back and stared at the ceiling. He replayed the events of the night. The most joyful time of his life. Sadia, her screams of pleasure. Her soft body. Her touch. Sadia, the woman of his dreams.

Where is Sadia now?

He saw her disappear. Transcend. Transform from physical shape to an ethereal one. She was happy. The happiest he had ever seen her. He knew things in his life were hard to explain, but where was she exactly?

***

July 25, 2018br

12:05 PM

He closed his eyes, thinking about all the things that

had transpired in the last 48 hours. Would he ever find answers? He opened his eyes and stared at the ceiling again; then he suddenly realized he was starving. He got out of bed and went downstairs to the kitchen. Everything looked spotless. Clean counter, neat dining table, shiny sink. The radio was on playing classical music.

He opened the fridge and looked inside. Besides some leftover roast and a few old vegetables, and what looked like expired milk, there was nothing else.

He sighed, closed the fridge, and decided to get some groceries.

He got out of the house and walked to his car. He drove to the nearest grocery store where he noticed that the parking lot was full.

Seriously? It's noon! Why is everyone rushing to get food! Don't these people have jobs to go to first thing in the morning?

He got out of the car and walked to the store. He
grabbed a cart and went down the first aisle he could see.
The store was playing an annoying song from the '80s.

Please stop this music.

Suddenly, he heard a loud bang. He turned his head
to see a young woman looking at a shattered pasta sauce
jar on the floor.

"I'm so clumsy," she said out loud.

Another woman passed by him. She was talking
loudly on the phone. "I told him to reschedule the
meeting," she snapped. "He never listens."

Jaxon couldn't tolerate all that noise around him.
Everything was getting louder and louder. He covered
his ears with his hands and shouted at the top of his
lungs.

"Stopppppppppppp it!!!! Be Quieettttttttt!!!"

All the windows in the store rattled.

Suddenly everyone and everything in the store,

including Jaxon, froze as if someone had pressed the pause button on a moving image.

The *inner* emerged, sliding seamlessly from Jaxon and stepping forward. As soon as he appeared, the *inner* stood tall. He shook his head and then turned around, facing Jaxon, who was still frozen like a statue. His face had a serious look.

"You need to relax, man."

A black Lab moved toward him wagging his tail. He gave him a pat on the back.

"What a good dog you are!"

He observed at least three dogs roaming around.

He shrugged, grabbed Jaxon's cart, and looked around at all the frozen people. For a split second he thought he saw a reflection of himself standing right in front of him, he wiped his eye and looked again but it was gone.

He pushed the cart and started walking toward a

young woman standing next to a toddler. They were both frozen, looking at the boxed juice shelf. The red-haired toddler had his hand on an organic apple juice box. His hair matched his mother's.

He approached them and brushed against the women's arm. A vision flashed in front of him.

He saw the woman sitting in a red fabric recliner in front of the TV, eating a bag of chips. She was watching a show about women fighting over a handsome bachelor. "No, no, don't kiss him," said the woman out loud. "He doesn't deserve you."

The toddler was sitting on the floor by her feet playing with Legos, building what looked like a castle. The woman put the bag of chips on the small wooden side table next to the chair and walked to the bathroom, leaving the toddler alone. "Mommy, where are you going?" he asked. "I'll be back soon, honey," she told him.

The woman went inside the bathroom, opened the medicine cabinet, and grabbed a bottle of oxycodone. She swallowed three pills without water. She looked at herself in the mirror, threw water on her face, then walked back to the living room to continue watching her show.

"I missed you, Mommy," said the toddler. "I missed you too," she said and then leaned down to kiss him on the cheek.

Mother of the year.

He kept on walking, dragging the shopping cart. He stopped by an older man frozen next to the cereal aisle. He was holding a cereal box and was looking intently at the ingredients. He moved closer to him. He was wearing khaki pants and a long red shirt. His glasses were sliding down his nose. With one hand the *inner* leaned on the man's shoulder looking at the cereal box. He didn't move. Instead, an image flashed before the *inner's* eyes.

He saw the man in a ballroom on a cruise ship. He was carrying his granddaughter, who was dressed in a blue princess outfit. She had a silver tiara on her head. There was a party going on. A band was on stage playing Latin music, and people were dancing. "Grandpa! I want to see the sea," demanded the child.

The old man walked with his granddaughter to the end of the ballroom toward the windows. He leaned by the window to show his granddaughter the vast sea. The girl leaned in, wiggled, his hands shook, lost their grip. She fell into the ocean. He screamed. Everyone screamed. The music stopped.

The *inner* quickly released the old man and shook his head. He had to forget that awful image. He suddenly felt his heartbeats in his throat.

The poor girl! The poor man!

He kept on walking through the store shopping until

he stopped in front of a couple holding hands. They were frozen in the canned goods aisle.

The woman had a red plaid scarf around her neck and was wearing a long skirt with a long-sleeved blue shirt. Her brown curly hair covered most of her face, but he could still see dark circles under her eyes.

What are you trying to hide with this scarf?

The man was wearing a pair of jeans and a T-Shirt that said, "Screw it, I need a beer." His arms were covered in tattoos. The *inner* touched the woman's hand. A vision formed.

The woman was in bed naked. The man was on top of her, fully dressed in faded blue jeans and a white T-shirt. He had his hands around her neck. "You're choking me," she gasped. "Do you like it?" the man asked, a cruel smile forming on his face.

"No, please stop," she pleaded. "Just wait. It'll get better," he said, squeezing harder. She screamed but he didn't stop. She begged. Finally in desperation she kneed him in the crotch and he screamed.

The *inner* let go of her quickly.

No wonder she was wearing a scarf, and what a monster this guy is.

He punched the monster in the stomach. He didn't move. He hit him again then again. Then gave him one last kick in the crotch and then kept on walking. He stopped in the bread aisle. He saw a silver-haired older woman in a wheelchair. She had a loaf of whole wheat bread in her lap. He walked toward her and touched her shoulder. A vision formed:

She was young, in her twenties, a ballerina dancing solo on a dimly lit stage. She was wearing a white tutu attached to a white bodice and she was stunning. She took a bow and left the stage to loud applause from the audience. The curtain went down as the orchestra kept playing. She went backstage where a man gently grabbed her arm and twirled her around to face him. He

took her head in his hand and kissed her passionately.

"You were amazing tonight," he whispered. "I love

you," she whispered back.

Wow. Life is so unpredictable.

The *inner* kept on walking. He stopped by a young

man with dreadlocks and a Rasta knit beanie. He touched

his arm and saw a vision.

The young man was on the sofa, a black dog curled

up next to him and a laptop on his lap. An email arrived

and his eyes lit up. "Finally, it's here," he told the dog.

He opened the email and read the first paragraph.

"Thank you for your interest in the position.

Unfortunately, we went with another candidate."

The young man closed the laptop and walked outside

to the small balcony. He tucked a couple of strands of his

long black hair behind his ear. He leaned by the railing

and looked at the street below. He heard the horn of a car

and the bark of a dog. He exhaled. He put his hand in his pocket and got out a pack of Marlboro Lights. He lit a cigarette. He inhaled, feeling the tobacco in his lungs. He blew out a smoke ring. "Everything sucks," he said out loud.

It'll get better, buddy. I promise.

Standing next to the guy with the Rasta knit beanie was a middle-aged woman with a phone balanced on her shoulder. She had short-cropped blond hair and was wearing a grey suit with black high heels. She looked like a senior executive at a Fortune 500 company. The *inner* walked toward her and touched her hand. He saw her.

She was seated a round table in a meeting room wearing a black suit and glasses with dark square frames. Around the table men in suits all stared at her intently. The only other woman in the room was a millennial, taking meticulous notes on a laptop. "Meeting adjourned," the woman said. She got out of her chair,

walked to the bathroom, went into a stall, locked the

door, and began to cry. The crying became fiercer until it

turned into wailing.

Things are not always what they seem, the *inner*

sighed. *I need to get groceries. I've had enough visions*

to last me a lifetime.

He zipped through the aisle while pushing the cart.

He finished all the shopping he needed in less than two

minutes. When he was done, he scanned the cart: cereal,

milk, eggs, bacon, ham, cheese, hotdogs, frozen waffles,

lettuce, tomatoes, asparagus, mayonnaise, and Mountain

Dew. He smiled. Everything he wanted was there.

He decided to take another stroll around the store.

That's when he saw him, a short, husky blond policeman

in a blue uniform, standing by the store's glass entrance

door. He was staring at something with a look of concern

in his eyes. He was frozen just like the others, but

something in him made the *inner* stop in his tracks.

What was this policeman doing at the store?

S. Sparks, his name tag said.

"I don't remember you being here earlier. Odd."

He got closer and stared at the frozen officer. He

decided to touch his arm and he saw that Officer S.

Sparks was there to arrest Jaxon.

The *inner* then walked back toward Jaxon and tapped

him on his shoulder. Jaxon woke up. He opened his eyes.

He looked at him intently.

"It's you. What are you doing here?" asked Jaxon.

"Just helping you out, man. I've already got the

groceries."

Jaxon looked inside the cart.

"Perfect. Thanks, man."

"We need to hurry, Officer S. Sparks over there is

here to arrest us over Sadia's disappearance."

Jaxon and the *inner* walked together to the self-checkout machine and paid for the groceries.

"I'm going to call it a day," he said as he slowly

began to merge with Jaxon. He took a deep breath,

grabbed the cart, and started heading toward the exit.

The store suddenly came back to life. People started

moving again and the noises resumed. The dog barking,

the child shrieking, the woman on the phone, the lady

pushing her wheelchair. Vanessa Williams' song.

We have to get out of here before it's too late,

Jaxon quickly pushed his cart and exited the store.

When he reached his car, he popped open the trunk

and quickly threw all the groceries inside. He got in his

car to drive back home, leaving the cart in the middle of

the parking lot.

He rolled down the window for some fresh air. He

felt invigorated.

"Later, Officer Sparks," said Jaxon out loud.

***

When he got home, he stocked all the food up and made himself a sandwich. He took it upstairs along with a can of Mountain Dew.

He went to his room, sat by his desk, and opened the lid of laptop. He decided to continue the research he started a couple days earlier. While munching on the sandwich, his brain scanned the information with the speed of light. Reading, digesting, absorbing. Hundreds upon hundreds of pages, thousands upon thousands of pages. He kept reading. He read and registered at a speed he had never experienced before.

He was not sure what he was looking for. He felt as if he was guided by an invisible force that compelled him to research non-stop.

To keep digging. There was something he needed to find. To unearth. He knew it. What was it?

Then suddenly, one thing stood out. An article about human evolution. It was written in the 19th century.

Jaxon read it once, then twice, then ten times, all in the span of ten seconds. He knew that he had already read a similar article before, but when? He had not researched 19th-century material before. It didn't make any sense.

He did quick research, and lo and behold, a very similar article was written by a different person but in the 21st century. The first article was written by someone called: R.C Wells, and the second one was by someone called Christopher Lu.

Here we are again?

Two completely different eras but they have the same writing style, the same energy? Is this guy immortal?

He googled his name. R.C Wells. The search results showed thousands of articles.

Could Christopher Lu and R. C. Wells be the same person? They have to be.

According to the internet, R.C. Wells was born in the 1800s.

Jaxon looked and looked but couldn't find a death date.

What's going on?

He felt his phone vibrate in his pocket. He took it out. It was Pete.

Why is he awake so early?

"Hey Pete, what's up?" said Jaxon as soon as he picked up the phone. He immediately put him on speaker, mesmerized by the search results. "You won't believe what I just found."

"Dude! Listen, you don't have much time. The police are looking for you," said Pete sounding panicked.

"Shoot," Jaxon muttered under his breath.

"Did you hear me? Two officers came to my house not too long ago asking for you. They just left. They're on their way to your house."

"What did they ask you about?"

"Sadia. One of her neighbors called them, said she's missing and that you had something to do with it. Did you spend the night at her place last night?"

"Yeah, but…"

"Wow. It's not like I didn't see that coming," he chuckled. "Where is she?"

"It's hard to explain over the phone," said Jaxon.

"What do you mean? Do you know where she is?"

"I do."

"Is she okay? Where is she?"

"She's, she's in a safe place. Don't worry."

"Just tell me where she is!"

"It's hard to explain," said Jaxon, whose voice started to increase in intensity.

Pete sighed. "Everything is hard to explain with you these days."

"Pete, I really don't need this now. I'm going

through a lot."

"I know, I know. I'm sorry. I just care about Sadia. You know?"

"You know I love her. I'll never harm her. She's safe. Don't worry and forget about the police. I'll deal with them."

"Okay, you just need to think of what you're going to tell them. They're on their way to your house right now."

"Thanks for letting me know. I'll handle it."

As soon as he hung up the phone, he heard the doorbell ringing.

They are here, that was quick.

On his way downstairs, he peeked his head in his parents' bedroom. He saw his mom sound asleep.

Good. The last thing I need now is mom seeing us get arrested.

He went downstairs and stood in the foyer.

What am I going to tell them? How am I going to explain the unexplainable?

He exhaled and walked to the front door and opened it. There he was: Officer Sparks.

Standing next to him was a slim woman with black hair tied up in a ponytail. She had black sunglasses. They both had their hands on their holsters.

"Hi, Jaxon"

Jaxon nodded.

"I'm Officer Sparks and this is Officer Vallas."

Officer Vallas looked familiar and after a moment Jaxon realized she was a friend of Sadia's family. He'd seen her at a couple of family functions. She looked upset, clearly worried for Sadia.

"How can I help you?" asked Jaxon, leaning against the door frame.

Jaxon could hear his heavy breathing. He was scared.

"We're looking for your friend Sadia. We have

witnesses placing you at her place last night. Were you at her place last night? Did you spend the night at her place?"

"Yeah. I did."

"I see. The neighbors reported hearing a loud commotion and seeing destruction to the property. Did you have anything to do with that?"

Jaxon's mind was buzzing. He felt hot all over and it felt like the world was tilting. Energy seemed to be building up in him and he didn't think he was going to be able to control it. His skin was crawling and it felt like he was going to explode.

"Well, yes and no. It's hard to explain," he muttered, trying to clear his head. All he could think of was the mounting pressure inside.

"Sir, please give us a clear answer."

Jaxon looked intensely at them. When he spoke it felt like he was doing so slowly, as though pushing each word out had suddenly become hard. "Listen, this is the best you'll get from me. I can't explain right now."

Officer Vallas stayed quiet, her hand placed on her holster as if she was ready to shoot any minute.

"Sir, this is serious," said Officer Sparks. "Sadia has been missing since last night. Do you know where she is?"

"She's fine," said Jaxon looking the officer in the eyes.

"Okay. Now we are getting somewhere," said Office Sparks. "Can you tell us where she is?"

He needed to move, to get away from the door. He needed to try and get a handle on what was happening inside him. It was like part of him was collapsing. Couldn't they see that? Didn't they know they needed to back off and give him space?

"Why do I have to tell you that? Why do I have to tell you anything? She's fine. Please don't waste your time on this."

The officer crossed his arms. "Listen, Jaxon, we have reason to believe that she's in a compromised situation and that you're the cause of it. You need to tell us where Sadia is. Otherwise, we'll have to take you down to the station for questioning."

"Leave me alone," said Jaxon grabbing the edge of the door. He was speaking as much to them as to the pounding in his head. He needed to think, to get clear, and he couldn't do it standing there talking to them.

"Sir, you need to answer our questions."

Jaxon screamed, "Leave me alone!"

"Sir. Can you please step out? You're coming with us to the station."

"I said, leave me alone!"

Jaxon closed the door with all his force, causing the two police officers to fly in the air off the front porch and fall on their backs in the front yard.

Why don't they just listen to me?

Jaxon felt even more hot and feverish, like a volcano ready to explode. What had just happened was only the beginning. He felt that. Something was changing and he couldn't control it. He went and watched the police officers from the floor-to-ceiling front window. Officer Sparks got up first and then helped Officer Vallas. They both had a perplexed look on their faces. Officer Sparks dusted himself off while Office Vallas put her hand on her back and cringed.

Officer Sparks grabbed his radio and asked for back up, then both he and Officer Vallas headed back to the police car, which was parked in front of Jaxon's house, blocking the driveway. Jaxon couldn't help but notice that Officer Vallas was limping.

I'm done with these morons.

Jaxon went upstairs to his room. He had to figure out what was happening to him. That was all that mattered now. He instinctively felt that Christopher Lu held a key

to understanding.

He went back to his desk and continued his research.

Christopher Lu! What's your story? How do you

know R.C Wells?

Ten minutes passed in which Jaxon had already read

20,000 articles. He heard a commotion outside. He

walked to his bedroom window and peaked. Ten police

cars were parked outside. At least ten officers wearing

SWAT gear were roaming around his front porch. They

were all carrying assault rifles. Four dogs stood by them.

It looked like a war zone.

He heard his mom come out of her bedroom. She

walked into his room. Her hair was messy, and she was

wearing black leggings and a gray wrinkled T-shirt. Her

eyes were puffy, and she looked as if she hadn't slept in

ages.

Jaxon bit his lip.

She's spiraling downward and it's all my fault.

"What's going on? What's all that noise outside?" she asked.

"Don't worry about it, Mom. I got this."

She walked to the window and looked outside.

"Oh my God, honey. What's with all the police? Are you in some sort of trouble?"

"Mom! let me handle it!"

She stared at him blankly for a moment then slowly nodded as though she were in a trance, and uncharacteristically she said

"You handle it then. I'm going back to bed."

Jaxon clenched his jaw. His felt sweat beads forming on his forehead.

He paced back and forth in his room as police, dogs, and more police cars surrounded his house. Loud police sirens went off.

"Too loud!!" shouted Jaxon. "My mom is asleep."

His phone started beeping—a text from the neighbor next door, a 16-year-old teenager who never left his room.

What's going on? Are you guys, okay? What's with all the police cars and all these dogs?!

All is well. I'm dealing with it, typed Jaxon. **They got the wrong address.**

Phew! Thought you were involved in some sort of a drug deal. Hehehe.

Jaxon put the phone back in his pocket. He clenched his fists. He felt he was losing his mind. He punched the wall next to the window. His hand went through it, creating a sizable hole.

He was enraged, like a savage animal. He couldn't hold himself together, hold himself back, anymore. He went downstairs, opened the door, and faced the army outside. His eyes were bloodshot.

"Get off of my lawn!" he shouted at the top of his

lungs and threw up his hand as if he was moving them out of the way. A huge energy wave was released from Jaxon. Everyone in the immediate vicinity including Jaxon, Jenna, Julius, the police, and even the neighbor kid all vanished, and the *inner* emerged. The oval shaped birthmark on his neck also vanished. The chain around the 8 point start pendent sparked, then melted and fell to the ground. Its purpose had finally been served. All the houses on his street shook. A couple of trees fell on the sidewalk. A few neighbors from down the block came out of their homes. Some were shrieking; others were in shock.

Mrs. De Carlo, who lived in the house down on the corner, came out of the house and stood on her front lawn. She was barefoot and dressed in a white nightgown.

"What's going on?" she called frantically.

"All is well. Just heavy winds."

"A tornado?" she asked.

"Maybe, but it's over now."

"The weather guy never mentioned a tornado."

"They never do! All is well, Mrs. De Carlo, you can

get some rest now."

"I saw some policemen outside. Where did they go?"

The *inner* scanned his surroundings looking puzzled

but calm. All the police officers were gone. Vanished.

All he saw were police vehicles! No more Officer

Sparks. No more Officer Vallas. No more gung-ho

SWAT, but there were four scared police dogs. They

were all barking, circling, and sniffing the grass, looking

for their partners.

There is no order without conflict. War is what makes all

worthy things stronger. Strength gives rise to order. So many don't understand this. So many flee in terror from the battles that confront them. They are weak, unworthy, without honor. They deserve to perish as quickly as the cherry blossoms they so often cherish.

Life is struggle. Life cannot exist without conflict. It is this very conflict that creates strength, resiliency, and perpetuates life. Each generation can only be strengthened if there is blood, fire, trial for the generation that has gone before. Without conflict to strengthen it, anything that lives withers and dies. Species that cannot fight, that cannot harness their power and control their environment, shaping it around them, go extinct. And so they should.

I have slain all my enemies, and some that were not. Now I find myself growing bored, restless. Without challenge there is nothing. Without the rush of the battle there is nothing. All things must find their opponent or else create one worthy of themselves. Long have I searched for something to challenge me, strengthen me, that I might grow and harness my power and emerge stronger, more powerful than any could imagine.

Now, I sense something. I can feel it calling out to me, a kindred spirit, a fighting challenge that fills me with a lust I have never known. I thirst for the battle. I long to test myself, push myself. Too long has it been since the heat of battle has been enough to stir me.

This new presence is something I have never encountered. The challenge entices, intrigues me. I do not know when this foe will emerge. I do not know the form it shall take, but I will be ready. I have honed every inch of my being and I will be prepared when the time is upon me. I shall not be taken unaware like a mewling infant in the night, seized by the tiger that lusts for its blood.

Battle requires strength, discipline, strategy, and patience. It is not enough to strike. One must know when and where. I will study my opponent as it draws near to me so that I may understand its strengths and weaknesses and counter them. I will be victorious. Victory rises from strength. Without it, a creature, a race, an entire planet dies and fades away. I will be strong. I will be victorious.

Chapter 8

Enlightenment

July 25, 2018br

4:04 PM

The *inner*, still standing outside of the house, observed his surroundings. He looked up at the clear sky and felt a cool breeze on his face. He inhaled a deep breath and let it out slow in a long sigh. He suddenly felt a sense of enlightenment, as if things were starting to fall into place to solve the complex puzzle of his life. He felt he was ready to accomplish a mission, his mission, willing to finally do what he was supposed to do, without any restrictions.

Jaxon is no more!

Starting from his heart, from his core, then traveling all through his body, a wave of energy shot out from him like a sphere. It flew out in different directions. His whole body shook as a bright light emanated from deep within his core. He let out a faint shriek. In an instant, the immense light engulfed everyone in his vicinity, erasing Jaxon's world in a flash. Everyone. The neighbors, the walkers, the joggers, the children. They all vanished, leaving nothing behind.

From the midst of the engulfing bright light emerged The *inner*, standing tall, taking it all in. He looked around him, at the people-free landscape that once housed Jaxon's world. It was all gone. All that was left were memories, memories of a life well-lived.

He suddenly felt an energy coming from inside his

core, drawing him, compelling him to move, to take a stride to the unknown, to keep finding answers.

He needed to unravel his true self.

Where am I going? I guess I will find out soon! Nothing has been predictable lately.

***

He kept walking and walking, compelled by the incredible force that pulled him. Part of him was excited; the other part was cautious, afraid even.

Am I being dragged to a guillotine? Or does paradise await me? Where am I going?

The energy field around him kept getting stronger and brighter. As he kept on walking, somehow he felt more vital to the world as the field around him got bigger and bigger. Everyone around him got erased, dissolving like melting snow. The neighbors, the

children on their bikes. Houses were left unattended,
animals were left wandering around, and bikes fell on
the roadside. The town where he grew up, the town that
once was buzzing with life, suddenly became a ghost
town—a no man's land.

Am I the only one?

He thought about his life. All of it, and then he
zoomed in on the past couple of weeks when everything
in his world changed forever, and there was no going
back. In his mind he replayed the significant events. The
accident, the horrible, horrible accident. Then the
unexpected event. Him separating from Jaxon, from
someone who housed him for as long as he lived.

He recalled merging again after experiencing the
taste of the life outside of a vessel. He remembered when
he first experienced it all for the first time. The smells,
the sounds, the physical touch. He recalled how he grew,
how he evolved physically and mentally. He recalled his

anger. His uncontrollable energy when he destroyed cars, property, smashing things, and caused the trees to fall. When he shouted at everything and everyone he came in contact with. He was a mess of anger and confusion. He was unbearable, untouchable, unapproachable.

Then he thought about the love of his life, Sadia. He thought about that night when their passion was finally consummated. Her moans. Her ultimate pleasure. He thought about when the unthinkable happened, when Sadia disappeared right in front of his eyes, melting within his veins, Sadia calming him, grounding him, making him whole.

And now this. Jaxon was no more. Gone forever. How could it be? It was a lot for the *inner* to absorb. What was really going on? He exhaled. Someone needed to give him answers. Who was he? What was he? What was going to happen to him now that he erased all of

Jaxon's world? The only world that he ever knew.

Jaxon's parents. His parents. Where were they now that

he completely extinguished them? Were they gone

forever? Would he ever see them again?

Why did he do all of that?

Inner kept walking, taking long strides, as the force

kept pulling him toward the highway. Cars were buzzing

around, exceeding the speed limit, and crashing. He

stopped by the highway's shoulder. He let out a sigh and

started erasing all the people. All the drivers. All the

passengers. Men, women, children. All disappeared.

Why was he doing that? Who made him do that?

Everyone disappeared. No one was operating the

moving vehicles. The cars continued rolling on their own

for a few seconds, and then he heard loud noises. Metal

on metal. One crash after another. Cars banging into

other vehicles. Cars veering off the road, hitting the

median. Cars flying in the air and crashing upside down.

One car caught on fire, then another, and another. The whole highway lit on fire. It looked like a scene from a war movie, from an apocalypse.

He kept on walking, erasing more and more. He heard screams of those who saw others vanish in front of their eyes. Screams pierced his ears. For some reason, that didn't deter him. He kept erasing more and more and causing more crashes, more destruction. More fire. Engulfing, hellish fire. He could hear the sounds of sirens approaching.

Someone called the police. They are going to be in for the shock of their life.

He smiled and kept on walking, erasing, deleting, and evaporating all the people he found on his way.

***

He stopped to catch his breath when he saw a light

emanating from an exit near the road. It was coming from a diner that had a giant pink neon sign. He kept on walking until he reached the entrance of the restaurant. He looked up at the sign.

"The Meeting Place," said the sign. He felt blinded by the light emanating from the sign, and he wanted to move on, to keep erasing everything around him, but he couldn't, as the force kept pulling him, and he had no choice but to step inside the diner. When he got inside, he was greeted by the smell of burnt burgers and brewed coffee. He looked around. The place had an 80's theme, pink and blue booths everywhere. Jukeboxes were on the table. Posters of Duran Duran and Madonna hung on the wall. People were dining, chatting. Babies were crying and toddlers were throwing tantrums. There were seniors, lovers, and school groups. The *inner* looked for an empty booth, but there was none.

What's so special about this place?

A bouncy song was playing from one of the many jukeboxes in the diner.

"Too loud," he shouted.

He clenched his fists as he sensed a stronger force of energy emanating from him. He scanned the diner. People started to evaporate right in front of his eyes. One by one, they all vanished. The adults, the kids, the toddlers, the waiters, the busboys. All disappeared into thin air—all except for one.

The *inner* closed his eyes and opened them again to make sure he was seeing what he was seeing. Right in front of him, leaning by the cash register, was a man who was indestructible, un-erasable. He took a couple of steps towards the man. The man was tall, fit with olive skin, and a rugged face. Around the man was what seemed to be a circle of bright light, that flashed for a second then dissipated. He was dressed in brown khakis and a plain white T-shirt. He was clean-shaven and had slicked black hair and thick eyebrows. Upon looking at him, the *inner* felt a sense of familiarity, of déjà vu, of coming home. He felt compelled to speak.

"What's going on? Who is this mysterious man? Why am I so drawn to him?"

He took a few more steps. The man smelled of the ocean, a smell that suddenly stirred all sorts of memories that were just out of reach. It made him nostalgic. It was a weird feeling that made him stop in his tracks.

"How did you do that?" asked the man, throwing his hands in the air.

"Do what?"

"How did you make everyone disappear like that?" the man said, pointing at all the empty booths in the diner with his index finger.

He shrugged. *"I'm not sure... I just do things, weird things."*

"Very curious," he said, shaking his head.

370

"Why didn't you disappear like the others? By any chance are we alike?"

"Hmm. We shouldn't be. I mean, there're only seven of us."

"Us?"

"Yes, The seven."

The seven?

The man ran his fingers through his hair. "I don't know, but there's something unique about you. Your energy. It's so familiar to me. How did you find me?"

"I was drawn to you by a force that I couldn't stop or fully explain. All I know is that it was like… a magnet. It kept pulling me, and I just knew I had to follow it."

"I see." The man tilted his head and looked as if he was lost in thought. "May I ask you something? "

"Yeah, sure."

"When did you come to be? And where were you born?"

The *inner* gave the man a suspicious look.

"Just indulge me, please?"

He cleared his throat. *"I was born on May 25th, 2000, in The District of Columbia."*

"Hmm... Who are your parents?"

"Well, they were Jenna and Julius Randle."

"Jenna and Julius… hmmm." The man got quiet for a bit. His pupils froze, and he seemed to be in deep thought. "Son of a gun!" He clapped his hands. "I know them. I know who they are!"

"You know them. Really? My parents? How?"

He exhaled. "It's a long story. How much time do you have?"

"As long as you want. I have nowhere to go now."

"Okay, let's sit," the man said, motioning for him to sit in one of the booths.

They sat across from each other in the booth. The man moved the dishes and the coffee cups that were already on the table to the side.

"Coffee?" he asked.

"Sure. "

The man snapped his fingers, and a waitress wearing a pink apron with the diner logo and a white hat appeared. She was short with long, light brown hair and freckles. Her name tag said, Gina.

"Hi, welcome to the Meeting Place. My name is Gina and I'll be your server. What can I get you to drink?" she asked, while handing them two menus.

"Two coffee, please," said the man.

"Certainly. Anything else?" she said.

"That's it for now. Thank you."

The *inner* watched the scene unfold with his mouth open.

"What the…? How did you do that? How in the world did you do that? "

"Do what?"

"Create that woman from thin air?"

"Oh, that. That's nothing. We do that all the time."

"We? The seven?"

"Yes, you're getting it."

"But how did you do that?"

"You may actually find out."

Gina came back with two mugs of hot coffee, placed them on the table, and cleared the dirty dishes.

The *inner* took a sip from the coffee. *Strong. Bitter*

"So," said the man, rubbing his hands. "First things first. Jenna and Julius are not really your parents."

"What? Are you sure? Well…. who are my parents then?"

"Well…. I'll explain."

"Can I trust you?" he asked, interrupting the man. *"What are you? Are you the scholar?"*

"It's your choice to trust me or not. I just am, and, no, I'm not a scholar. I know all of this because I was him for a night."

"You were who?"

"Julius!"

"How So?"

"Well for us it's easy," said the man.

The *inner* decided he was willing to hear him out. He thought to himself, *Let's see where this is going.*

The man took a deep breath. "I guess I'll start from the beginning. In the early beginning, when this planet was in its infancy, there were only seven of us." The man took a sip from his coffee. "We existed alone before the arrival of any plant life or animals."

"I've read about this 7 in my research. Are you suggesting you were the first people on earth?"

"Exactly, well not people but Life?"

"How can that be true? I mean, you would have to be... how old are you?"

The man smiled. "I'm ancient."

"You don't look it,"

"With our existence also came immortality, other life on this planet somehow chose reproduction. They were able to multiply while we stayed only 7."

"Interesting."

"We age but not the way other life on this planet does. We age as the planet ages, and as time passes we grow in power and ability. We were the first sentient life on this planet, the first to become self-aware. Over time, one by one we found each other, initially not knowing how to speak. Eventually we learned basic communication skills, hand motions, writing. We began to form words that grew into a full language.

"We noticed as life started to form on this planet, we were the strongest, the fastest, most intelligent. Some of us grew territorial and extinguished other life like the dinosaurs and then all Homo Habilis in its infancy." He paused and stared at this coffee cup. "Some of us have regrets for what was done, but we pushed forward and things were never the same." He sighed. "Over time our powers grew massive, and so out of control that we could no longer remain in close proximity to each other. So, we all set out in different directions, but maintained a special mental connection. We found that we each had control over a fundamental element that shapes this reality. I control Mass and Energy."

The *inner* leaned back in his booth. "*Wow! this is a lot to take in. Is this real, or are you telling me a fairy tale?*"

"Of course, it's real, and in time you may be able to verify it all for yourself. Just wait. There's much more." The man cleared his throat. "We decided to name the land we inhabited Pangea, to us it means home. With our uncontrollable abilities, storms broke out, natural disasters, hurricanes, earthquakes, volcanoes erupted, reality distorted, time shifts and space fractures occurred.

We felt that in our current state if we didn't separate, we would undoubtedly destroy the planet. So, we all decided to go in seven separate ways as far as we could go. Shortly after, our combined force separated the mass of land into eight different parts."

The *inner* nodded his head. He suddenly felt that the man was telling the truth. There was this warmth about him that made it hard for him to distrust him.

"What happened after?" he asked as he started to feel invested in the story. He wanted to know more. He needed to learn more.

"Well, things took a turn," said the man as he firmly gripped the rim of the coffee mug. "The eighth mass that was known to us as Atlantis sunk, and then only seven remained. The man fidgeted. "We were lonely, and when you are lonely, you can either build or destroy, so we built."

"Built what?"

"Mentally connected we used our will to create the first energy constructs."

"What are these energy constructs?"

"They are reflections of our inner self, manifested into a physical form."

"Like Gina, the waitress?"

The man smiled. "Exactly."

"Can you show me how you do that again?"

"Okay." The man snapped his fingers, and a man appeared in front of him. He had dark skin and black hair and was wearing black pants and a white long-sleeved shirt.

"Hi, my name is Jose, and I'm the manager of The Meeting Place. I just want to make sure everything is going well."

"Yes. Great coffee," said the man smiling.

"Let us know if you need anything, and enjoy your evening," said Jose, then walked toward the kitchen.

"Amazing."

"You think? I'm used to it. I forgot what it was like to see it for the first time."

The *inner* looked at his fingers and then snapped them. Nothing. He snapped them once, twice. Three times still nothing.

He looked back at the man. *"Are you saying that everyone on this planet is a construct?"*

"Yep!"

"Including my parents, family, and all my friends?"

"Yes, them too!"

The *inner* felt his heart skip a beat. *"Even my parents? That just feels so wrong. For so long I was so attached to constructs. They raised me, guided me, cared for me and all along they were just mere vessels?"*

From the corner of his eye, he could see Gina and Jose chatting amicably by the kitchen counter. Gina laughed and twirled a strand of her hair behind her ear.

380

Jose touched her shoulder

"Are they flirting? Do these constructs know what is going on around them?"

"Are you okay with all this?" asked the man.

"Yeah, I suppose I have to be. I'm just thinking about the constructs. They just seem so real to me."

"Well, kiddo, they are real, just not like you or I. They were created in our image and likeness. They are as real as we willed them to be, along with all that they create."

"Just curious. What exactly went into creating the constructs?"

"Well, different things contributed to that. We created them from our own emotions, our aspirations, feelings, desires, ambitions. A piece of who we are is within them."

"I'm Listening."

"Let's play some music, shall we?" said the man.

"You look so solemn. This is not a funeral. We need to lighten up the mood a bit. Let's see," he said as he fumbled with the jukebox, which was placed on the table. He put in a quarter.

"Lollipop, Lollipop" started playing.

"I love this song," said the man smiling. "Where were we? Ah! The constructs began to populate this planet with different versions of themselves, ourselves, with part of us within them. It's hard to tell the difference nowadays. Some of them actually look identical to us. They are so, so complex."

"How so?"

"At the time we had no idea the constructs could interact with one another. They copulated and produced, creating more versions of themselves. To us that was completely unexpected."

"The constructs could reproduce and the seven never could?"

"We never have, we tried and tried, different combinations but they all failed, so we believed it wasn't possible."

"Interesting, how is it possible that I came to be?"

"I'm getting there. We only knew we had the ability to create constructs, but they took things a lot further than we imagined."

The man rubbed his chin. "They created fire and eventually tools, they built homes, and built buildings. They cultivated land, created metal. They created boats, planes, submarines, spaceships; you name it. Some even created weapons and started wars."

"The seven created the constructs, and then the constructs created this utopia?"

"Exactly," he nodded. "It became almost fun and quite shocking to see how different they were from us and to see what they would do next."

"I bet. It's like watching a show."

"Yeah, something like that. You know, we were quite content with what we created, but our constructs were not satisfied. They kept wanting more. They kept growing, kept reaching higher."

"That's quite the story, but that doesn't explain who I am and why I was drawn to you."

"Well, there is another caveat to the story," said the man. "Let me get some more coffee." He motioned for Gina and asked for more coffee. She came back in a few minutes with a new pot of steaming hot coffee.

"Okay, where were we?" he said and took a sip of his coffee. "What's the matter?" the man asked, looking at the *inner*, who turned his attention to Gina and Jose.

"Nothing, I can't stop thinking about the constructs. I mean the two that you just created so easily."

"Are they distracting to you? You need to stay with me." The man waved his hand at Gina and Jose, and they both disappeared right in front of their eyes.

"See, you're not the only one who can vanish people," said the man with a smile.

"I see," he smiled back.

"Anyway, where were we? Yea, so we, the seven, found that we can enter our energy constructs, and feel what they feel, be who they are, and move throughout the world undetected, if we choose to."

"I've experienced that. It can be overwhelming, exciting, and unexpected."

"Indeed. It was a game-changer for us. It gave our lives a new meaning. The ability to enter a construct and see their entire lifetime, and actually be a part of it, was the most unexpected gift. As I think back on the events, I guess when I was your father another one of us was your mother at the same time, and we unknowingly conceived a child. The child must have been you, which makes you my son!"

"You're my father?!" he asked, feeling his hands

trembling.

"Yes. This has never happened before. You're the only offspring. You're unique. One of a kind, the 8th!"

8th felt his heart skip a beat.

This man is my father? My biological father, and I'm the 8th!

He suddenly had a heavy feeling in his stomach. He took a deep breath,

"I'll never forget the day I saw Jenna," said the man. He grabbed a sugar packet and melted it in his coffee mug. "She was radiant, so pretty. When I met her, there was something about her energy. It pulled me to her. There was no way I could let her go."

"*Well, Jenna is pretty inside and out,*" said 8th. "*I have been lucky to have her as my mom.*"

"That night we made love."

Oh, a frown formed on his face. He couldn't imagine his mom making love to that man, to a man who wasn't

Julius. The thought made him sick to his stomach.

"I remember everything about that night," said the man.

"Okay. Okay. I get it. Can we move on?"

"It's tough to see you now and not think about Jenna, you know."

"Okay, I get it."

"Well, you know what, I think it's time for you to meet the other six."

"The other six?"

"Yeah. I'm sure they have already felt your presence."

"You think so?"

"Of course. You felt my presence. Didn't you?"

"I did."

"Well, I'm sure they could feel yours and would want to meet you."

"I'm ready, a little nervous though."

"Nothing to worry about, for the most part we're all logical, although some can be a little eccentric," said the man smiling. "And besides, don't you want to meet your mother?"

"My mother?"

"Yeah, your real mother."

"I'm just a bit overwhelmed," he said shaking his head. He felt his head was about to explode. He clenched his jaw and started grinding his teeth, as his inner power built up enormously.

"That's normal—a lot to take in. But don't worry. I'll help you along the way. I'm your dad, after all."

"Yeah. My dad. It feels weird to say it out loud."

"You gotta get used to it, kiddo."

"I'll try."

"And now is a good time for you to start your training, before you inadvertently destroy this continent, with all that power."